Fortnight on Maxwell Street

Fortnight
on Maxwell Street

David Kerns

Bay Tree Publishing, LLC
Point Richmond, California

Library of Congress Cataloging-in-Publication Data

Names: Kerns, David, 1944- author.
Title: Fortnight on Maxwell Street / David Kerns.
Description: Point Richmond, Calif.: Bay Tree Publishing, LLC, 2018.
Identifiers: LCCN 2017048170 | ISBN 9780996676533 (pbk.)
Subjects: LCSH: Medical students--Fiction. | Inner cities--Fiction. | Slums--Illinois--Chicago. | Poor--Illinois--Chicago. | King, Martin Luther, Jr., 1929-1968--Assassination--Fiction. | Chicago (Ill.)--Fiction. | GSAFD: Autobiograpnical fiction. | Historical fiction.
Classification: LCC PS3611.E763 F67 2018 | DDC 813/.6--dc23
LC record available at https://lccn.loc.gov/2017048170

This novel is dedicated to Gayle Kerns,
my indispensable partner and first reader.

Fortnight on Maxwell Street is a work of fiction inspired by real people, whose identities, words, thoughts and actions have been invented or reimagined for the sake of the story. The narrative depiction of James Earl Ray combines journalistic precision, where possible, with ample flights of dramatization that have no factual basis.

Contents

Screw your courage to the sticking place.
—*William Shakespeare*

No realistic, sane person goes around Chicago without protection.
—*Saul Bellow*

Part One

Day One

To the clatter and whack of tire chains and wiper blades, Doctor Butler steered her red Buick Roadmaster down the crunchy black tracks of an otherwise snowbound side street. The buildings left and right were a monotony of weathered three and six flats, slumlorded brick tenements that were once the fine apartments of thriving immigrant families, long since gone to their preferred neighborhoods and suburbs.

Nick Weissman was in the back seat wedged between Mary the midwife and Carla the nursing student. His classmate Jeff Peerce was riding shotgun. Nick asked, "What about our orientation?"

Butler told him not to worry, that they'd finish it later. She sounded New England, though she'd been working out of the Near West Side of Chicago for almost half a century, delivering babies in buildings you wouldn't walk into if you had a choice, which these two senior medical students did not. "When we get up there, don't touch anything," she said. "Just watch me and Mary. You'll get plenty, believe me." She cracked the window and lit her third Chesterfield in twenty minutes. Nick got the March morning air like a scalpel, then the sweet sulfur of the matchhead, then the smoke. Those who could—and Nick and Jeff certainly could not—called her Butts.

Out of the car, the two young men each carried a black leather instrument bag the size of a small suitcase. Carla schlepped a foot-high pile of newspapers, while Butler and Mary, the pros, walked ahead unencumbered. Butler's stride and bearing were all business, her bright red go-go boots a snappy non-sequitur.

"C'mon, c'mon," Butler said, herding them through a front door into a barely warmer lobby of mailboxes and buzzers. The tile floor was filthy, sticky. Of the six doorbells, not one was labelled. Butler was about to try one when a boy, he looked about eight, appeared at the top of the first flight of stairs.

"You from the maternity?"

"That's right, son," Butler said.

He waved them up and led their little caravan into the dark.

Nick thought about his Jewish mother and her hand-me-down prohibitions—the perils of swimming after eating, of going outside with a wet head. If she knew where her twenty-four year old son was at that moment, she'd have probably asked if he was trying to kill *her*.

Butler told them to try not to breathe. It was too late for Nick. His stomach roiled with the reek, a mélange of urine and feces and rotting garbage that saturated the stairwell. At the top landing, Butler was shooing them into an apartment like a basketball coach, her left arm extended and pointing into the open doorway, her right windmilling. "Let's go, let's go, let's go."

Inside, the flat was a surprise. There was the aroma of baking, an olfactory antidote, Nick figured, for the stench of the building. And there was the smell of Lysol. They were in the living room amid old but serviceable upholstered chairs, needlepoint pillows and walnut tables covered with white tatting. There was a black spinet overflowing with sheet music. The floor was polished oak, and all four walls were covered with family photographs. The place was a home.

They were welcomed by a calm and gracious dark-skinned woman, young enough to be the mother-to-be. She had a big afro and wore black horn-rimmed glasses. "Willa, my daughter, she's in the bedroom." She told them that Willa's pains were five minutes apart and that her water had just broken. Then she offered them coffee and pastry.

"Miss Brown, is it?" Butler asked.

"Yes, May Brown."

"Well, thank you for your hospitality, but right now I think we'd best get to evaluating Willa. Is that the bedroom?"

Butler led them in. The small room was crammed with their crew of five, mother May, two mid-twentyish women who referred to themselves as the *ahn*ties, and Willa, looking every bit her fifteen years. From a single bed in the corner, she looked up at Butler.

"Are you gonna help me?"

Butler told her that she would, that they would.

"Would you cover my feet?" Willa asked.

She re-positioned the girl's baby blue polyester blanket, squaring it to the foot of the bed and across the teenager's chest.

The queasiness in Nick's gut was gone, replaced by the itch of apprehension. Protected and supervised, for the time being he was not in jeopardy. But he knew that soon enough he would be in a place like this or much worse, on his own.

Willa whimpered and said, "Help me." She had a flattened hook nose, bulgy brown eyes, and acne dotting her café-au-lait skin. Her hair, bunched into short and disorderly rubberbanded braids, was oiled.

"What's your name again?" Butler said, looking at Nick. He told her for the third time in as many hours.

"Well, Weissman, we're going to examine this girl. Come over here and help get her into position." Then she retrieved Jeff's identity and assigned him to the opposite side. Nick and his fellow student, a millimeter from doctorhood, survivors of the brain-stuffing, sleep-depriving, debt-encumbering eight year pre-med and medical school marathon, were now going to be stirrups.

As they slid her buttocks to the bottom edge of the bed, Willa was exposed from the ribcage down. Her abdomen bulged in the shape of a watermelon from her breast bone to just above her genitals, the taut skin shiny and bisected by a brown-black line of pigment—the *linea nigra,* Nick remembered—running top to bottom.

He looked across at his colleague. Like Jeff, he had one hand under a thigh, flexing the knee and pulling it toward his chest. They had Willa splayed, ready for Butler's lubricated glove.

Suddenly Nick swallowed a laugh and was not at all certain he'd be able to contain the next. In this first clinical adventure with Doctor Teresa Butler, the Medical Director of the Chicago Maternity Center, a cackling outburst would have been about as welcome as booming flatulence. Still, looking at Jeff, he could not get the image out of his head. Though it had happened over three years earlier, it remained a contender for the most macabre and hilarious of medical school moments, no small distinction considering the collective comedic guilty pleasures of the Northwestern University Class of 1968. Jocular sublimation, anxiety cum merriment, a gallows doozy. He feared he would snort.

It was the fall of freshman year and he and Jeff and two other green souls were being introduced to the art and science of physical examination on a surgical ward at the Chicago VA Hospital. Their teacher, a urologist no doubt in the snare of tedious academic obligation, paraded them with faint exuberance from one patient to the next, pointing out physical findings and asking questions as they strolled. There were hernias and enlarged prostates and kidney stones. And there was a case of acute epididymitis, a red-hot and swollen crown of tissue sitting atop the testicle, a condition you unconditionally did not want. Eventually they came to a patient, or rather to a pulled curtain concealing a patient, who got a somber preamble. "This gentleman," their guide said quietly, "with carcinoma, cancer of the penis, had his amputation about ten days ago. Let's have a look."

Now had Jeff simply fainted, it would have been an acute embarrassment, short-lived grist for the sadistic kibitzers—there were plenty in the class of '68—but that would have been it. What made it legendary was that upon witnessing the unfortunate man's hideous leftover, Jeff collapsed unconscious upon him, pelvis to stump. Then, in what looked like a scene from a madcap movie, they were simultaneously peeling their entirely limp colleague off this horrified and quite specifically limp patient, expressing frenzied and preposterous contrition, all the while laughing hard enough against clenched mouths and noses to clear their sinuses for a month.

Thankfully Jeff, with an armful of Willa's leg, remained upright and Nick somehow managed to control himself. Butler stepped between them, her right hand gloved and wet with soap bubbles. She lowered her chin and looked at Nick over the rims of her round wire spectacles. "Boiled soapy water. Best sterile lubricant out here in the field, and everyone's got it." Then she leaned forward, her ears even with her patient's knees. "Okay, let's see where this baby is."

Willa emitted a barely audible grunt and Nick looked down just in time to see Butler removing her gloved index finger from the teenager. The woman had completed her assessment in the time it took him to start getting his nerve up.

Butler startled him, shouting inches from his ear. "She's

fully effaced, eight centimeters."

Mary the midwife bellowed back from the living room, "Where do you want to do this?"

Butler stepped back, took a visual measure of something between Willa's legs, and made her decision. "Kitchen table." Without looking up, she kept Nick and Jeff in play. "You two go watch her do the setup."

Mary was on the living room floor rolling newspaper. "It's for leverage," she said. With a four-inch thick newspaper roll in each hand, one rolled the long way and one the short, she got up and led them into the kitchen. "Okay, gentlemen, wash your hands and get masked, capped and gowned. This is our maternity suite." Nick may have been only three months from his M.D., but this nurse was giving orders and he was taking them.

Mary narrated as she covered the kitchen table with overlapping individual sheets of newspaper from the remaining pile. "These are sterile, you know. Newsprint is sterile." She unfolded an oilcloth drape and placed it over the newspaper, two-thirds on the surface of the table, the remainder hanging almost to the floor at what would obviously be the business end of the setup. Using safety pins, Mary shaped the hanging end into a trough. "If we do this right," she said, "we'll keep the mess to a minimum. Find me a small pail or a wastepaper basket."

Butler hollered from the bedroom, "This girl's about ready, are we?"

Mary looked at Jeff as he fiddled with his paper cap and mask. "Tell her two minutes."

Carla the nursing student took a bucket from under the

big-basined porcelain sink and handed it to Mary. She set it at the foot of the table where it received the oilcloth trough. Then, quickening the pace, she laid a large white bedsheet over the oilcloth and executed a rapid series of folds using the newspaper rolls, leaving them at right angles to one another inside the sheet. Mary saw that Nick was perplexed. "You'll see," she said.

"Well, ready or not." It was Butler right behind Nick. She had Willa, her huge abdomen bulging out from under a sleeveless cotton top, under one armpit with Mother May under the other. Mary took over from May, and she and Butler lifted Willa to the table, knees up and apart with her feet firmly against one of the concealed newspaper rolls.

Willa was moaning. "Hold me, somebody. Hold me."

Butler quickly scrubbed her hands at the sink, then snapped on a pair of pale yellow rubber gloves. Without being asked, Mary took a small piece of white adhesive tape and fixed the nosepiece of Butler's eyeglasses to her forehead.

"C'mon, fellas." Butler was gesturing the two of them to close ranks on Willa. "Just control her knees. Don't let her close up on me."

Willa continued to moan. "Put me asleep, please, can you put me asleep?"

Mary held out a stainless steel bowl containing wads of gauze floating in sudsy water. Butler took them, one at a time, and began prepping Willa. "You start at the center and work outward. You never come back, then you throw it away." She scrubbed as she spoke, dropping one wad after another into the bucket below.

Willa was panting, throwing her head to one side, then the other. "Oh god, help me, help, help." Then she quieted and tried to roll on her side.

Butler leaned forward. "When you get a contraction, dear, do you feel like pushing?" Willa shook her head. "Now take two breaths in, then let it out. You're doing fine. You just rest for now, go easy now, just breathe in and out real easy now."

The crusty schoolmarm of an obstetrician, her voice clipped and severe a moment earlier, was now nearly melodious in quiet and soothing guidance. From Nick's vantage point at Willa's left knee, he watched Butler's face soften and her attention focus, as if now that the preliminaries were over—the arrival, the introductions, the laying out of equipment and supplies, the scrub and prep, the near completion of labor—it was time to get personal.

"She's all covered with sweat," Butler said. "Let's get a cloth and wipe her face."

The contractions came, wrenching, about a minute per, punctuated by two or three minutes of exhaustion, Willa panting and pleading, Butler in warm and steady command.

"You've been a real good girl. Do you want a little water to drink?"

"I can't, I can't. Please help me. Please."

"You're having a hard time getting this little baby out. I wish you could tell me when you feel like pushing or not. Can you?"

"Oh god! Help, help me. It's hurting. I can't, I can't."

"Look, let me take your hand."

"Can I turn over? Please, please, please."

"Easy now, dear, just stay with me. Push down hard. Another deep breath and then push again."

"Wait, wait, wait, wait. My right leg hurts."

"Hold it longer, longer. That's the way, longer, longer."

Nick lost his grip as Willa suddenly straightened her left leg. "Now don't jump," Butler said. He got her back in position.

Then, over the next several contractions and breathers, Butler somehow cajoled and mesmerized this unprepared teenager into the alternating rhythm of pelvic agony and blessed rest. Like an obstetrical lion tamer, Nick thought.

"Alright, let's see where we are," Butler said. She did another digital exam, but this time she lingered. "We're occiput posterior, face up." This meant that the back of the baby's head would travel along the floor of the vagina. Nick knew that this was the hard way out, slower and more painful.

Butler dropped the maternal persona to sum up with her students. "So we've got an immature primip with a posterior presentation. I doubt we'll get by without forceps and an episiotomy. And she'll need a pudendal block."

This was suddenly anything but assisted natural childbirth. She'd get nerve injections through the vaginal wall, then a skin incision from the vagina downward toward the rectum, and finally an extraction using metal tongs on the baby's head.

"If you were on your own at this point," Butler said, "you'd definitely be calling the OB resident for help."

"Are the OB residents available, you know, immediately

available?" This was Nick's first question of the rotation.

"Well, of course," Butler said, as if he'd asked her if the sun were yellow, as though this were a question that had not for years bedeviled the Department of Obstetrics or burned through the student grapevine.

Now Nick was grafting ominous flesh onto his fearful bones. He kept his mouth shut and thought about the discouragement wrought the week before by his classmate and buddy Don Greenberg.

Nick had never seen anyone who looked quite like Donnie Greenberg, his pronounced roundness and bulbous nose, thin and scraggly blond hair, and a goofy and boisterous *joie de* everything; a clown without need of costume or make-up. Donnie's rage, then, in full combustion across the table from him, was all the more disturbing.

"It was the single worst fucking thing that has happened to me in medical school," he said.

They were a block from Northwestern at Guido's, the Chicago pizza landmark and a cherished med student hangout for decades. The pizza and beer punctuated and mollified the insane hours and workload. Days away from his own inner-city trial-by-fire, and scared well beyond acknowledgement, Nick had asked Donnie to meet him to talk about his time at the Maternity Center. It didn't take him long to close in on his catastrophe.

"The OB resident on call was Westerman," he said, "the prick from Passavant."

Nick had done his junior obstetrics rotation at Passavant

Memorial Hospital and knew the guy, an imperious jerk two years out of internship.

"We're on our own, me and a nursing student, in this roach-filled flat with a woman who's blood pressure had gone through the roof," Donnie said. "I phone Westerman and he starts pimping me with his Socratic bullshit. I tell him he needs to come see the woman. He says there's no emergency. I say she's not responding to meds. He tells me the woman's not in active labor and I shouldn't be bothering him. I tell him I'm very, very worried about this mother and baby. He says, Greenberg, I'm not here to take care of your anxiety. I wanted to fucking kill him."

What happened next was the stuff of nightmares. When the woman did go into labor a few hours later, she developed full-blown epileptic seizures and coma. Donnie wound up carrying her down three flights of stairs with the intention of driving her to the hospital himself. At the pavement, a late-arriving ambulance—he'd called ten minutes earlier—took her to Cook County Hospital. He thought the mother survived, but was uncertain about the baby.

"As far as I'm concerned," he said, "I was fucking abandoned."

So much for *joie*. In search of someone to ease his misgivings, Nick had come to the wrong guy.

Butler held a trumpet in her left hand, the so-called Iowa Trumpet, a six-inch stainless steel needle guide. It got its name from its horn-shaped mouth into which one introduces a long needle, in this case for the purpose of numbing Willa's genitalia. Nick had several supervised stabs, so to speak, at this procedure during his junior obstetrics rotation at Passavant. With a gloved finger and working blind, you find a particular bony landmark along the vaginal wall, use it to position the guide, and slide the needle in for the anesthetic injection. An important nerve—the pudendal—is "blocked," chemically rendered non-functional, and the patient is successfully numbed. On his first pudendal adventure, Nick managed to twice drive the long needle into his index finger, resulting in yowling pain, bleeding, obliteration of sterile technique, and high entertainment for the surrounding nurses, residents and attending physicians.

Teresa Butler smoothly executed a block of Willa's left pudendal nerve, then her right. "Let's give it a minute to take," she said, folding her gloved hands in her lap. The teenager was between contractions and for the first moment since their arrival, no one was speaking or even moving. The five of them—Jeff, Nick, Mary, Carla and Butler—formed a tight circle around Willa's lower body. Mother May and the aunties filled in about her head and shoulders. May held Willa's right hand in both of hers. The little brother, the one who led them up the stairs, had been whisked off to a neighbor. This makeshift delivery room was ready, clinically and emotionally. Butler's technical skill and demeanor, at once commanding and comforting, made this happen. By reputation, this had been the case for decades. Nick's clear appreciation of this, however, would have to wait. At Willa's side, his attention had its fill just trying to please and not falter as an assistant, while continuing his negotiation with dread. He could not know, much less regret, that this was one of the few times he would see Teresa Butler, the sole master of their fortnight, in action.

Willa did not feel the episiotomy, a three-inch incision which opened the way for the extraction of her baby. Butler gave the blood-wet scalpel to Mary and asked her for the forceps. "I'll bring him out face up," she said. "No choice." She'd somehow decided it was a boy.

Mary handed Butler the forceps, paired concave metal blades designed to fit on each side of the head and face. Applied one at a time, they then interlocked like scissors, allowing forceful traction on the baby's head. The first time Nick saw them, he thought they belonged in a medieval museum.

"Monitor the fetal heart rate while I do this," Butler said to no one in particular.

Carla had the only free hands. "One forty-four," she said.

Nick was surprised to see Butler drop to her knees as she began the delivery. She narrated for their benefit, a nearly whispered instructional commentary. This was interspersed with out-loud commands and encouragement for Willa.

"When the contraction starts, you pull straight for the ceiling. If it were face down, you'd pull toward the floor. Okay, here we go. Now, honey, you've got to help me. Now push hard, push. Once more now, push hard, push hard. You put all four fingers around the forceps and pull up. The traction is steady and continuous, not jerky. Push for me dear. Don't stop, keep pushing. Here we go, here we go."

First he saw only hair, black, wet and matted, then a pale blue and wrinkly little face. The forceps came off.

"Okay, no cord around the neck. Suction the mucus out." Mary complied with a little red rubber bulb syringe to the baby's nose and mouth. This elicited a cough, but no breath. "I've got it on the sacrum and I'm rotating it 180 degrees. Push now, push. See, I'm not pulling on the neck, I'm reaching in and pulling on the shoulders. Now push hard, push. Once more now, push hard, push hard."

The head and neck were out and the baby had rotated face down.

"Now let me show you how to deliver a shoulder. Look, he's taken his first breath."

In a few seconds the chest and abdomen were out and Willa lifted her head, startled at her first child's first cry.

And then, "We got a boy, we really got a boy!" Butler held him up for everyone to see. "Okay, let's get the cord clamped. Oh, that's a big baby."

Mother May and the aunties laughed and Willa blurted, "I don't know about no second one."

In quick and quiet order, the umbilical cord was cut, Carla pivoted with the newborn to the kitchen counter, Mary took the lead to deliver the afterbirth and Butler, walking away, yanked the tie of her paper mask with one hand while reaching for her smokes with the other.

Nick and Jeff, the leg holders, continued to stand there like spear carriers in a high school play. It's an odd thing, this almost doctorness—physician impostors, menial laborers, competence and confidence all over the place and not by a long shot reliably in synch. Nick's confidence at the moment was woeful. It wasn't just that he was not adept at forceps delivery. He wasn't even supposed to be. It was that he was not at all certain that on his own he would have even recognized that this was a complicated labor. Butler's rectal exam and easy diagnosis of the baby's dilemma might have been for him not just a literal poke in the dark. Had he been alone with Willa and failed to recognize her jeopardy, it would have come down to luck, the ill side of which was fetal distress, or worse.

Every one of his student obstetrical experiences had been closely supervised—the next one would not be. Yes, he'd delivered six healthy babies in his junior rotation, but each was chaperoned, safeguarded by hovering guidance, competence at the ready. Northwestern prided itself on its supervision and protection of the medical students, but that was at its private and prestigious core—at Passavant, at Wesley Memorial, at Evanston Hospital. In the out-lands, places like the Chicago Maternity Center or Cook County Hospital, it was the Wild Midwest. Cook County was particularly notorious for its huge volumes of indi-gent patients and its unsupervised doctors-in-training. A Northwestern faculty member famously said that at Cook County Hospital a surgical resident could do two hundred gall bladders *wrong*. How many deliveries could he do wrong? How much trouble could he be in before he even knew it? Would he, like Donnie Greenberg, find himself in over his head without promised reinforcements, a novice with the well-being, or very life, of a baby or a mother at stake?

Standing there, a bit player with no lines to speak and

no actions to take, Nick was grateful for his last moments
of irresponsibility, of safety.

The Center

His body was back in Doctor Butler's Roadmaster, but Nick was lost in thought, replaying the woman's easy professional command and its opposite, his obvious inexperience and wobbly insecurity. He took little notice of the grinding traffic, the sun-lit afternoon's melting snow, the Sunday bargain hunters on Maxwell Street. Butler pulled into the one vacant Chicago Maternity Center parking space, directly in front of the main entrance and labeled 'Medical Director.'

Jeff and Nick were led inside through an empty patient waiting area and up a flight of stairs to a small conference room which was, to be generous, utilitarian. In disarray were a dozen or so metal-legged school chairs, the kind with a laminated writing surface that folds up and to the side. Two of these were already occupied by the third and fourth of their medical student quintet, Jim Fisher and Larry Berlin. A Kodak carousel projector sat atop three telephone books facing a blank white wall. Teresa Butler stood next to a flip-over green chalkboard on wheels, which looked like it hadn't had a decent washing since the Korean War.

"Where were we?" she asked. "And isn't there supposed to be a fifth student?"

There was indeed. Bobby Plunkett was hours late. Their medical school class had only a few unreliables, and Bobby was not one of them.

They'd been slogging through their Maternity Center orientation when Willa Brown's labor pains intervened. Butler picked up where she left off, with the distribution of a deluge of photocopied instructional packets—the rules and regulations for their two weeks of obstetrical boot camp—accompanied by a running commentary of emphatic reminders of this, prohibitions about that, caveats, pearls of wisdom, simple advice. It was a mountain of information: protocols for everything from cutting infant toenails to treating life-threatening maternal hemorrhage, forms for prenatal care, for tracking the details of labor, for creating a birth certificate, inventories of home delivery equipment, instructions for how to mix baby formula, how to get reimbursed for a taxi ride to a delivery, how to get rid of a placenta, how far to roll up your sleeves for an pelvic exam (two inches above the elbow!). There were dozens of handouts and hundreds of details. It was important and it was necessary, but it was indigestible, like the proverbial sip from a firehose. When Butler finally finished and Mary showed up to give them a walking tour of the place, it felt like mercy.

Once Butler was gone, Larry Berlin told Mary that

they were missing a medical student. She made a comment about Plunkett's rear end, two hands and a treasure map. Though not at all evident during Willa Brown's delivery, this was a funny midwife.

Mary led the four of them through the building. They began on the lower level, half above ground and half below, which housed all of the patient areas—registration, waiting, and a cluster of examination rooms. The second story was for staff, including offices, the conference room from which they had just fled, and a kitchen/dining area. The top two floors were residential, exclusively for the visiting nursing students, most of whom were from St. Olaf's College in Minnesota, and strictly, they were twice told, off-limits. As Mary showed them around, she talked about the history of the Chicago Maternity Center.

The place was founded on Valentine's Day 1895 by Dr. Joseph Bolivar De Lee, whom she described as a world famous and pioneering obstetrical lunatic. It was initially named the Chicago Lying-In Dispensary, then for over a quarter of a century the Maxwell Street Dispensary, and finally in the early 1930's the Chicago Maternity Center. Its motto was "Safeguarding Maternity," its mission in brief: to give high quality care to the poorest of women, and to teach doctors, students and nurses the art and science of obstetrics. Over its seventy-three years of service, the Center had provided home deliveries for 140,000 babies and trained 12,000 physicians and 13,000 medical students. It was by far the largest and most ambitious program of its kind in America.

Nick and his fellow medical students knew that home

deliveries were hardly groundbreaking. They'd of course been universal for most of humankind, and were nearly so at the turn of the twentieth century. In 1932, when the Center adopted its modern name and established its affiliation with Northwestern University Medical School, two-thirds of all mothers were still delivering at home. After World War II, with dramatic advances in infection control and anesthesia, obstetrics shifted to the hospital setting. By the winter of 1968, less than five percent of American women were delivering at home.

"Our moms are better off delivering where they live," Mary said. "For them, it's that or Cook County Hospital. Where would you rather be? Our outcomes are better than County, and have been for decades." She reeled off the statistics, and you could tell from her ease that this was a regular spiel. At Cook County, the maternal death rate was four per 10,000 live births. In the Center program, from 1955 to 1961 there were 18,000 consecutive home births without a single maternal death. At County, the infant death rate was 26.7 per thousand live births; at the Center 14.5, roughly half.

Jeff asked if that was because the Center was so good or because Cook County was so bad. She said, "Both." Then she told them to get their coats. They were going outside.

The weather had changed. The sky was solid gray, the Lake Michigan wind cutting cold. Still, the block was abustle with the overflow from the famous outdoor market on Maxwell Street, which ran along the south side of the Center. They reached the end of the building on the market side, then circled back toward the main entrance.

Architecturally, it was a typical Chicago institutional structure, small red-brown brick and mortar with large vertical rectangular windows, three to a story on the short side and twelve on the main side facing Newberry Street. The entry was a double glass door under a glass transom. The place looked more like a school or a police station than a health center.

"This is staff parking," Mary said. She was pointing to three spaces, each occupied, facing in toward the building. One of the vehicles was Butler's Buick.

Larry asked Mary if it was safe. "You'll meet Ernie," she said. "He's our Matt Dillon. Nobody bothers the cars."

About twenty yards behind Mary, from the direction of the street market, Nick saw their missing medical student walking slowly toward them. Bobby Plunkett wore an orange thermal vest over his white cotton hospital jacket, and carried an overstuffed duffel in one hand and a small black doctor bag in the other. A cheerful sort, his expression foretold something else. He waited until he was standing among the five of them and said, matter-of-factly, the last thing Nick wanted to hear. "I just got mugged."

Nick was a Chicago boy, streetwise enough to err well on the side of caution, particularly in that part of town. And that was before he heard the grapevine tales of brutality to the Maternity Center's doctors, nurses and students. Officially, people talked to the med students about being smart, being careful, but nobody told them about specific assaults that had occurred over the years. It turns out there were plenty—hold-ups, muggings, even stabbings and shootings. Three years before Nick's arrival, the Dean of the Medical School issued a directive that all Maternity Center comings and goings be accompanied by police. This was unmentioned in their orientation—written or verbal.

The broken down part of town around the Maternity Center, the Near West Side, was tough turf. It certainly wasn't the only dangerous area in the inner-city—one could get conked on the head, or worse, in dozens of Windy City neighborhoods in 1968—but it was as dangerous as any. And it was, like the entirety of the inner West and South Sides, almost all black.

The Negroes, as they were referred to in polite company in the 1950's, came to Chicago in three waves, starting with a small nineteenth century migration of businessmen and professionals. They settled in a South Side corridor near the lake which became known as the Black Belt, and they were ambivalent at best about their poor, uneducated brethren who were to follow. The two subsequent huge migratory waves were the Great Migration from the South during the First World War, which was largely in pursuit of jobs that had been vacated by the soldiers fighting in Europe, and then the massive flight from the continuing indignity of Jim Crow Dixie in the 1940's and 50's. Between 1940 and 1955 a half million Blacks came up the Mississippi River Delta to Chicago, settling almost exclusively on the South Side and the West Side, where they encroached deeply into established Jewish neighborhoods.

Jews had come to Chicago in two waves, first the German speakers from central and western Europe in the mid-nineteenth century—educated, secular and often professional. They settled along the lakefront north and south of downtown, were accomplished in business, and identified as much with gentile well-to-do Germans as with their Jewish *landsmen*. The much larger second wave came in the last decades of the nineteenth century and the first decade of the twentieth. Unlike their predecessors, who tended to hold them in low regard, they were in flight from the pogroms of Eastern Europe, poor and poorly educated, avidly religious, and Yiddish-speaking. They came mainly to the West Side, often settling first in the Maxwell Street neighborhood and then migrating west to Douglas Park and Garfield Park, exactly the migratory route that Nick's family had followed.

While the West Side Jews held on to their property—their businesses and their rentable and ultimately slumlordable apartment buildings—they residentially fled en masse to the lakefront, to far North and South Side neighborhoods, and to the northern suburbs. This was their generation's great migration.

At age twenty-four, Nick was confident of his open-mindedness, his lack of prejudice, his 60s credentials. No one had ever alleged or even hinted that he had done or said something that was racially biased or bigoted. Had they, he would have righteously, indignantly, defended himself. Still, in his hidden spaces, his reptilian places where primal instincts incubate and fear and the reflex to survive rule the unconscious roost, he was a conventional creature, afraid of the un-him. It's not that he wanted to actively harm or belittle black people. He was, in fact, a liberal, which was just fine in those JFK-LBJ days. He had marched, for goodness sake—for school integration, for civil rights, for voting rights. He may have hated the war in Southeast Asia, but he loved the war on poverty. He dug the wit of Dick Gregory, the dignity of Rosa Parks, the passion of James Baldwin, the audacity and courage of Muhammad Ali.

He was raised by a black woman named Effie Smith, well half-raised. She came all day five days a week to his family's West Side apartment, to cook and clean and take care of his sister and him. This was commonplace in their Jewish middle-class culture, whether moms were employed or not—and most moms, including his, were not. Effie was treated as one of the family. She ate at the table, shared in family celebrations and gift-giving, went along on vacations. She was valued and always addressed respectfully. Still, in her absence, his parents called Effie 'the girl.' At least they never called her the *schvartze,* a word his mother abhorred. His father, however, used it in reference to other people's domestic help, as well as for pretty much any other black person on earth. His mom shushed his old man about this for the entirety of their fifty-seven year marriage.

Nick's prejudice was fearful, not hateful, and it was specific. He was afraid of black male strangers. In his defense, he was taught to be. He was told that they might be dangerous, that they might have knives or guns. The West Side and South Side ghettos were forbidden ground. You would never choose to walk in those neighborhoods, you didn't even want to drive through them. Carjacking wasn't yet a word much less an urban epidemic, but the prospect of a brick through the windshield was deterrent enough. There were exceptions, though. It felt okay in a crowd—on Maxwell Street on a busy Saturday or Sunday, at Comiskey for a Sox game, at the Chicago Stadium for the Blackhawks or the Bulls. He'd even gone with his high school pals to the black blues clubs. Those adventures were something else again, spine-tinglers, the scared shitless price they were willing to pay to see and hear geniuses like Muddy Waters and Howlin' Wolf and Little Walter.

He'd known from the start of medical school, for almost four years, that his two week rotation at the Maternity Center was required and inevitable. He was not panicked or obsessed with worst-case scenarios about personal danger. His anxiety was mostly about screwing up medically. He was thinking about obstetrics and grateful for a break from the traditional grind of student rotations on the hospital wards. He looked forward to having a huge learning experience and surviving this remarkable cultural-professional immersion. Still, there was a quiet physical fear, a simmer, one part common sense discomfort on those authentically mean streets, one part paranoia amid dark skinned bogeymen. And Bobby Plunkett wasn't helping.

"You just got mugged?" Nick said. It wasn't a question, it was a plea for detail.

"Well, not *just,*" Bobby said. "I've been with the cops for the last two hours."

This was a hell of a way for their full team of five—Bobby, Jeff Peerce, Jim Fisher, Larry Berlin and Nick—to spend its first moments together. They could have walked twenty yards and listened to Bobby in the warmth of the Center, but this tale wouldn't wait. So they stood out there in the cold, hands in their pockets, shoulders scrunched, every icy breath easily visible.

"I was walking here from the Halsted el station," Bobby said. "I figured it'd be safe in broad daylight on a Sunday afternoon."

Nick was certain that his face plainly betrayed his thoughts about his classmate's judgment. Bobby had decided to walk alone through nearly a mile of one of the most dangerous slum neighborhoods in America. It was a wonderment to Nick how people smart enough to successfully run the medical education gauntlet could be so breathtakingly stupid. Bobby was one of a horde of solid Midwestern blondies in his med school class—small town, palefaced, straight-laced, Bible Belt super-achievers. He'd never met these people until he went 'Downstate' to Champaign-Urbana for undergrad at the University of Illinois. In his Chicago public high school, a crazy quilt of Ellis Island progeny, there'd been exactly none.

"I was walking past this empty lot," Bobby said, "and I saw something out of the corner of my eye. Then I smelled alcohol."

Bobby was surprisingly calm. Nick's heart was pumping enough blood for both of them.

"The guy was reeking. He was behind me and he pushed something hard into my ribs. He told me to stop moving."

"Was it a gun?" Jeff asked.

"I guess," Bobby said. "I don't know, I never saw it."

If he'd had a stethoscope in his ears and a reflecting

mirror on his forehead, Bobby could not have been any more conspicuously a medical professional. With his white coat and black doctor bag, he was unmistakeable. The conventional wisdom was that if you were obviously a doctor on duty, you'd get safe passage. So much for that.

"He told me to give him my wallet."

"Not your doctor bag?" Larry said.

"That's all he wanted." Another urban myth shattered, that muggers are all junkies, that they're after your needles and drugs. "He took the money out and threw the wallet on the ground. I told him I was a medical student, that I was here to deliver babies, to help the families in the neighborhood. You know what he said?"

Nick was half-listening. Maybe it wasn't really a gun, maybe the man was just bluffing. He wanted to believe that. He was scared and trying not to show it. He'd been in fistfights in his life, years before in the seventh and eighth grade and in high school. He'd been shoved and punched and even kicked. But he'd never faced a deadly weapon. It was one thing to imagine the possibility, but this had just happened, this was too damn close for Nick's comfort.

Still inexplicably cool, Bobby finished his story. "What the guy said was, you oughta be more careful, doc, this is a bad neighborhood. You believe that? And he just slowly walked away."

"With your money?" Nick asked.

Now his corn-fed classmate got to look at Nick like *he* was an idiot.

Night One

It was like a firehouse. Poker and bridge and monopoly and TV and Top Forty and chess and noshing and naps and bull sessions and crosswords. And waiting.

"Two cards," Nick said.

"Pair and a kicker, right?" Larry Berlin liked to kibitz as he dealt.

Nick was second up. Jeff was out with one of the nurses on his first home delivery, Jim Fisher would get the next one, and then it would be Nick. They were in the two story brick residence, their student quarters on West 14th Place, three long blocks from Maxwell Street and the Center. It was officially known as Booth House, but everybody called it "the barracks."

Fisher tossed four cards away. "Probably keeping the bullet," Larry said.

Plunkett was stretched out on a brown corduroy chair and ottoman in front of the TV, a tabletop portable with rabbit ears. He had a lapful of pizza and Ed Sullivan was feeding straight lines to Lucille Ball.

Larry smirked and tap-tapped his cards with his index finger. "I'll just play these," he said. Away from the poker table, he was not a particularly annoying guy.

A big steam radiator against the wall clanked every few minutes as if someone were banging on it with a pair of pliers. It worked, though, and thank goodness it did. This living room, their safe harbor and social hall for the next two weeks, was about as cozy as a meat locker. The floor was linoleum, wall to wall. With the exception of the corduroy chair and one small sofa, all the seating was hard molded plastic. The flimsy curtains helped but you could feel the March chill a foot from the windows. Still, if you stayed away from the drafts, you could hang out unbundled.

The first floor of the building was community space— this main living room, a kitchen, and some storage. Each of them had a small bedroom on the second floor, and there were two bathrooms to share. Likewise, there were two telephones, one up and one down. During the night it would be the responsibility of the next person "up" to answer the phone. It was likely, though, that every call was going to wake every one of them.

Later that first evening they watched news coverage of the anti-war presidential candidate, Eugene McCarthy. "Our stated objectives in Vietnam are in reality different from our practical ones," the Senator said. "We proclaim that our ultimate purpose is support for self-determination, to let the people of South Vietnam work out their own future, free from foreign interference. In reality, we have interfered in South Vietnam and have continued in power in Saigon a government dependent upon the United States."

About halfway through the show, Jim Fisher got the call from the Center and Nick was glad to see him go. He was pro-war and his condescending comments about McCarthy were starting to piss him off.

Nick was no pacifist, he just thought that the domino theory for Southeast Asia was misguided and dangerous. A popular history professor at the University of Illinois had indelibly influenced his view of the Cold War. He convinced Nick, and a horde of others, that the defining struggle in the world was north-south and not east-west, anti-colonial and not ideologic. He was the first person Nick had ever heard say that the United States government overrated and overstated the world communist threat. It was, at the time, startling.

With Fisher on his way, Nick was first up and nervous. He left his bedroom door ajar so he'd be certain to hear the telephone. The upstairs part of the building was about as homey as the rest—tile floors, bedsheet curtains and flimsy mattresses on heavy metal frames. On his night table was a book, *Joseph Bolivar De Lee: Crusading Obstetrician,* a biography of the 'lunatic' founder of the Center they'd just heard about. It was written in 1949 by De Lee's colleague and friend Dr. Morris Fishbein, who for a quarter of a century had been the editor of the *Journal of the American Medical Association.* He began to read and within a page the exhaustion of the first day of their fortnight washed over him. It stole his attention and, for a little while, his anxiety too.

He'd slept about five hours when the phone rang, and ready or not—medically or testicularly—he was going down the obstetrical fire pole. Doctor Butler had told them in their orientation how these home deliveries were triaged and triggered. The calls from the community came in through the Center switchboard which was staffed round-the-clock by operators who responded by strict protocol. If the information indicated that a woman was definitely or even possibly in labor, the caller was transferred to the nurse at the top of a duty roster. The nurse had the responsibility to classify the case as simple or complicated, and assign it appropriately—to a medical student only, to a med student accompanied by an obstetrical resident, or in the most complex cases to a med student and a fully-trained attending obstetrician. If she was uncertain about this decision, she could phone the resident or the attending physician on call for advice. Once the composition of the team was set, she made a decision about transportation—private car, taxi or the police, depending on the staff involved, the hour, and the danger of the destination. By the time a medical student was fetched at the barracks, the team and the equipment were in the vehicle.

It was just before dawn and Mary and Nick were in the back seat of a taxi on their way to Garfield Park, a crumbled neighborhood about three miles west of the Center. "Our patient's name is Helen Jackson," Mary said, "and Helen's a grand multip." *Multip* was common medical shorthand for multiparous, which referred to women who'd had two or more live births. Grand multip was a term reserved for women who had successfully delivered at least five babies.

He asked Mary how many kids Mrs. Jackson had and she answered in conventional lingo. "She's a G14, P11." The G was for *gravida*, which is latin for pregancy, the P for *para*, a twist on *parere*, which means giving birth. They were coming to relieve this woman of her fourteenth pregnancy, and she had already delivered eleven live children. Helen Jackson was multiparous by a mile.

Twenty hours earlier, walking into May Brown's tenement flat, Nick had braced himself for a sad and seamy expectation—of squalor, destitution and dependency—and he was dead wrong. In the Jackson apartment, he got to be woefully right. They were assaulted, first, by the acrid and unmistakable stink of urine decomposing to ammonia. He'd smelled this before, the scent of soggy neglect of the very young and very old. There was also something fetid and sour which Mary crisply diagnosed. "Rodent crap."

The front room was a disarray of mismatched and disintegrating upholstery, makeshift cardboard carton tables, strewn clothing, and dull and damaged toys. They walked past a bedroom and Nick saw something which compelled him to enter and which, he was certain, altered the calculus of his conscience. At age twenty-four, he had his declared and unripened philosophy, his liberalism. He cared about poverty, at least the idea of it, but he had no personal experience of scarcity, of fundamental need. He had never even authentically witnessed it. In that room were four children on a double bed, three laying the long way and one crosswise at their feet, but that was not what burned itself into his awareness. Four more children, younger ones, were in a doorless closet asleep on separate wooden shelves. Each, bundled in tattered layers of towels, blankets and coats, was secured by a rope looped through a wall hook. In this modern American city, two-thirds into the twentieth century, the room looked like the hold of a slave ship.

In the next room they found their patient wide awake in bed, and to Nick's disappointment still quite pregnant. Though he didn't let on, he'd hoped that this would be a MUD, a Medically Unattended Delivery, a reprieve. Given Helen Jackson's history, she might have easily spit this baby out before they got there. The correct medical student attitude was a consuming commitment to hands-on experience, to racking up procedures of all kinds, including deliveries. As a junior student in obstetrics, in the safety of the hospital, he'd wanted all he could get. But on the scary precipice of his Maternity Center baptism, even with the prospect of a 'just catch it and try not to drop it' newborn, even with Mary the talented midwife as back-up, he would have been grateful for a postponement.

They'd been greeted and escorted by a skinny, polite middle-aged black man in pajamas and a worn flannel bathrobe. His speech was slow and careful and faintly slurred. He called himself Mr. Jackson, and when he introduced them to his wife, Nick could tell he was from Louisiana by the soft way he said *matoinity*.

Mary didn't so much let Nick take the lead with Helen as force him, remaining silent several feet behind. He was accustomed enough to independently initiating with patients, though not without occasional rookie lapses. His most embarrassing and preposterous gaffe had occured a year earlier at Evanston Hospital, an eminently proper and private suburban teaching institution. He was the junior medical student on thirty-six hour duty for general surgery, and aching for sleep hours after midnight. The charge nurse paged him to evaluate a woman who was having post-operative pain in her abdominal incision, and when he got the call he was also getting an insistent and increasingly uncomfortable call from his bladder. It was a stone's throw to the patient and about a hundred yards to the nearest men's room, so he decided to tough it out. Upon entering her room, he intended his cheerful opener, "Hi, I'm Doctor Weissman. I'm here to take a peek." What he said was, "Hi, I'm Doctor Weissman. I'm here to take a leak." He could not say which of them was the more horrified.

Nick managed his initial exchange with Helen Jackson without foolishness, and her immediate description was unnerving. She said that there was something wrong, that she was having hard labor "but this child ain't goin' anywhere." From a Willa Brown—a first delivery, a teenage *primip* with a torrent of frightened and inexperienced grievance—this would have drawn little attention. He knew, though, that when a seasoned grand multip like Helen tells you something disturbing about her labor, you'd better listen.

As he began taking a medical history, Mary went into action, documenting pulse, blood pressure and respirations, and opening the supplies he would need, notably gloves and lubricant. Mrs. Jackson, half-sitting against a pile of pillows, struck him as weary—not just sleep-deprived, labor pains tired, but years weary. She answered his questions with scant vocal or facial expression. When two of her sons burst in and were hastily shooed away by Mr. Jackson, Helen gave no indication that she noticed. She was obese, unkempt, and could have easily passed for ten years older than her stated thirty-six. When it was time for her pelvic exam, she pulled her knees to her chest and unceremoniously exposed herself, with the detachment of long lost vanity.

The pelvic examination, like the assessment of the heart, the eye, the nervous system, demands technique and art, skill and touch, and years to refine. Nick's facility at pelvics was similar to most of his classmates—amateur to adequate. The evaluation of someone in labor is focused on the state of the cervix, the opening of the uterus through which the baby makes its expulsive journey into the outside world. The characteristics of the cervix that matter—its thickness and the size of its opening—are best determined by direct palpation with a lubricated glove, usually two fingers, in the vaginal canal. That's the easy way, at least for the doctor. The medical students, however, did it the hard way. It was thought at the time, at least by some, that a rectal exam was safer, less likely to cause bacterial contamination and possible infection of the newborn. His task, then, was to place one lubricated, gloved finger into the rectal canal and make an accurate asssessment despite the presence of both the rectal wall and the vaginal wall between his finger and the anatomy of interest, the cervix. It was hard enough the easy way.

He placed his left hand on Helen's abdomen, on the dome of her bulging womb, and his right index finger into her rectum. In that position, with the patient on her back, the cervix lies above and should be appreciated by palpating forward and upward. He did so and could discern, well, nothing. He continued to silently discern nothing for another twenty seconds or so and then removed his finger. He must have been easy to read because Mary was already putting on a pair of gloves.

"I think there's maybe a foot," Mary said. She looked up at the ceiling and closed her eyes, concentrating. "I really think there's a foot."

Nick repeated his exam, this time vaginally, and felt it easily. Instead of an infant skull pushing its way through the cervix, there was the soft flesh of baby buttocks punctuated by an unmistakable dangling little foot. In parlance, this was a single footling breech presentation, and they needed help.

"Pick a card," he said, "any card at all."

Two of Helen's boys, about ages eight and ten, were sitting on the living room floor with Nick, while Mary, with Mr. Jackson in tow, was trying to transform a wreck of a kitchen into an acceptable delivery room. The resident on duty was on his way. Unfortunately, it was Grant Westerman, the jerk who'd left Donnie Greenberg high and dry with his convulsing patient.

Nick fanned the deck and the older boy pulled a card. "Now show it to your brother," he said, "remember it, and put it back anywhere you want."

He'd never seen a breech delivery, but he understood the danger to these babies. There was concern about compression of the umbilical cord, but most of all there was the risk of injury to the so-called "aftercoming" head. Critical decisions had to be made about the necessity for Cesarean section and the use of forceps, and miscalculation could be harmful, even lethal. These babies had a 3-4 times greater mortality rate than the head-first variety.

Nick turned away from the boys for a moment, and when he turned back he dropped the deck of cards to the floor. All but one landed face down.

"Is that your card?" he said.

The younger boy looked at him with perplexed delight. "How'd you do that?"

"It's a magician's secret. I can't tell you." The kids asked for another card trick, then another, and his meager repertoire was just about shot when the one-man cavalry showed up.

Grant Westerman was an archetypical surgeon—physically big, confident, action-oriented, domineering—the kind of person who made Nick certain that he didn't want to go into a surgical specialty. It was unfair, of course, to stereotype specialists. Neurosurgeons were not necessarily instrument-throwing maniacs, orthopedists not invariably dumb jocks, pediatricians not always bowtied weenies. Still, there was a tendency for the shoes to fit, and, specifically, plenty of grapevine evidence that this particular senior obstetrical resident was an overbearing bully. It turned out, though, that he was better than that. And worse.

Westerman strode in and took over. In quick succession, he examined Helen, inspected the kitchen, and gave Mary a series of instructions. He addressed Helen as Mother, Nick as Doctor—this with unmistakeable irony—and Mary respectfully as Mary. Even the most pompous of physicians understand that you don't alienate invaluable senior nurses.

He surprised all of them when he extracted a small baby doll from his briefcase and took Nick aside for a tutorial.

"You're going to deliver this kid," Westerman said. "Mother's a grand multip and likely to be easy. I'll do the nerve blocks, but that's it." He told Nick that he would talk him through the breech delivery and take over only if necessary. Then he used the doll, a classic with long lashes and rolling blue eyes, to demonstrate exactly how Nick was going to bring Helen Jackson's twelfth living child, albeit backwards, into the world. As he taught, he softened, quietly explaining and showing hand positions and the direction of traction. Nick's questions were answered directly and without condescension. Westerman was even reassuring. "Don't worry. You'll do fine." Nick hadn't expected that kind of support. He wasn't sure what to make of the guy, but he knew that he felt less anxious than he did a few minutes earlier.

Helen was taken into the kitchen and they got down to business. The setup was basically the same as for Willa Brown, though the surroundings beyond the clean perimeter were wretched. The sink was piled high with encrusted dishes, the garbage can overflowing, the windows filthy. The spokes of the grates atop the gas stove were caked with congealed yellow fat, each greasy radial array looking wierdly like the foot of a giant chicken. Despite the putrid surroundings, Nick focussed on the patient and the task at hand.

"Okay, Mrs. Jackson, just rest between the pains, just try

to rest." He knew he was emulating Teresa Butler and her melodic guidance. Westerman was to his immediate right doing pretty much the same thing for Nick.

"Now gently tug on the foot," Westerman said, "and see if you can get the leg fully extended." Nick had it between his index and middle fingers and was able to bring it through the vagina and into view. It was in the expected orientation, with the heel up and toes down, and it was pink. This baby was coming out feet first, on its belly, and with plenty of oxygen in its tissues.

Helen Jackson made little fuss with her contractions. She grimaced and sweated and forcefully exhaled, but otherwise barely made a sound. Nick told her not to push yet, that he'd let her know when. As Westerman had instructed, he reached under the baby as far as he could and swept his hand down the chest and abdomen in an attempt to deliver the second leg. It worked. Now he had two pink little feet protruding from Mrs. Jackson.

Mary was to Nick's left preparing supplies and instruments. She asked, "Are you planning on an episiotomy, doctor?" Anticipating the delivery of the baby's shoulders, Nick told Mrs. Jackson that "we" would push with the next contraction, and that after that we would deliver the head and we'd be done. Helen had nothing to say but Mary repeated her question. "Doctor, does she need an episiotomy?"

The senior resident elbowed Nick in the ribs. "She's talking to you." He'd heard the question, but with Westerman present he couldn't imagine that she was addressing him, a mere medical student. Besides, he didn't know the answer, or rather he didn't know he knew.

"I'm not sure," Nick said.

Westerman did a quick Socratic exercise with him, classical positive roundsmanship, demonstrating that Nick did in fact know the answer. This grand multip had stretched out to accommodate the heads of eleven previous babies, and almost assuredly would accommodate this one. There would be no elective episiotomy. In the worst case, one could always do a last-minute incision, a "controlled tear," if it appeared that the patient was about to uncontrollably tear. Prodded with the right questions from Westerman, he knew all of it. Then, just as quickly, the big resident took him down a peg.

"Okay, move over," Westerman said. "It's time for the nerve blocks. I'm not turning you loose with a six-inch needle in a vagina full of breech baby."

He did the pudendal anesthesia as effortlessly as Butler, and then he restored Nick front and center. The preliminaries were over, it was time to deliver this baby. Nick asked Mary for the one essential he would need, a large sterile towel. With the next contraction, and a good deal of assistance from both Mrs. Jackson and Nick, the shoulders came through. Now only the head was undelivered, the largest part of a newborn's body and subject to the most serious injury. Exactly as Westerman instructed, and was instructing still, he supported the baby lengthwise—it was a girl—her chest and abdomen lying on his left forearm, and wrapped the towel around her trunk and arms for warmth and traction. His left hand, palm up, extended inside the vagina and slid under the infant's face until his fingers came to rest on her cheekbones. His right hand, palm down, was on the baby's upper back. He extended the index and middle fingers on each side of the neck and curled them over the tops of her shoulders. He had control of her, now all he had to do was get her out. Westerman was quietly coaching him all the way. Nick was hoping they could do this in one contraction.

"Mrs. Jackson, please tell me as soon as the next one starts."

She didn't speak up but Nick could tell from her eye contact that she was with him. Westerman moved a few steps forward to Helen's side and choreographed the finish. "With the next contraction," he said, "I'm going to push down on the baby's head through her abdomen. It'll keep her head in flexion, that's critical. Mary, you monitor the heart tones. Doctor, you keep the face and head steady with your left hand and just pull toward yourself and down with your right. Mary, if she gets hung up, we go straight to the forceps, but I don't think it's gonna happen."

Then they just stood there for about a minute. Nick thought that Mary could have monitored his own heart tones without a stethoscope.

"Okay," Helen said, "I'm gettin' it."

"Here we go," Nick said. "Now push and keep pushing." He did exactly what Westerman instructed, pulling out and down with his right hand. "Push, Mrs. Jackson, just keep it up. Push, push, push, push."

It happened faster than he expected, and there he was with a new baby girl in his arms. With Westerman pushing from above and Nick pulling from below, the head easily slid under the pubic bone and out into the world. Mary reached over with a rubber bulb syringe and suctioned the nose and mouth. The infant choked and sputtered and coughed, and then she wailed. They cut the cord and delivered the placenta in short order, and presented the baby to Mrs. Jackson. She held her with one hand on her chest, and seemed neither happy nor disappointed. Her touch was gentle, but she said nothing. Nick watched to see if she would align her face with her new baby, the instinctive mammalian bonding position about which they'd heard so much. She didn't. There was nothing about Helen Jackson's appearance or behavior that suggested this was anything close to a blessed event. She was, he thought, joyless, resigned to her relentless maternity and miserable surroundings.

Nick, on the other hand, felt pretty good. Sure it was a grand multip, and yes, Westerman gave the anesthesia and called the shots at the very end, but he delivered the newborn, a breech without complications. This was a personal first and certainly his biggest obstetrical accomplishment. He was one for one for the fortnight, relieved, and proud.

He examined the baby, gave some standard instructions about postpartum and pediatric follow-up, and was helping Mary clean up and pack the instruments and supplies. Westerman, who'd been unexpectedly gentle and supportive, was within earshot telling Mrs. Jackson that he was arranging for her to have her tubes tied. She had not made the request, nor had she been asked or counseled. He had brought along an authorization form and was insisting on her signature. Nick looked at Mary and she averted her gaze to the instruments. Mrs. Jackson, without question or comment, signed it. Nick thought that, given her circumstances, tubal ligation made sense, though Westerman's approach violated everything he'd ever been taught about informed consent. Mary told him later, in the taxi back to the Center, that Westerman did the same thing after every Maternity Center delivery. She said that if Grant Westerman had his way, every poor minority woman in Chicago would be sterilized. And Nick had been starting to like the guy.

Nick

In grammar school, the kids called him Nicky the Nig. His hair was pure black, low on his forehead, his eyes the color of dark chocolate. His skin, a blend of bronze and olive, was stark evidence of his mother's Sephardic bloodline, and a joker's delight on the playground. The kids thought it was funny to tease him, and Nick pretended that he didn't care. But when he looked in the mirror, the taunt would emanate from within, and with a viciousness not conveyed by his schoolmates. *Nigger!* He hated the way he looked and wondered if he could be fixed, somehow lightened. By seventh grade the kids had knocked it off, but Nick had not. Over the years his hurt and angry inner voice became more muted, but the seeds of shame and self-consciousness had been planted. For Nicolas Alexander Weissman, green-brown was not, and would never be, beautiful.

His mother's father, Abram "Abe" Barron, was born in Thessaloniki, Greece, the country's second biggest city and home to its largest population of Jews. Most of these Sephardim had migrated centuries earlier from Spain, once again running for their lives as they had been since the parting of the Red Sea. In 1905 Abe made his way to America as a teenager, to the West Side of Chicago, speaking Greek, which was useless among the Ashkenazi of his new neighborhood, and Ladino, the exotic Spanish-Hebrew tongue of his ancestors. The latter helped a bit with the Yiddish speakers, but Abe needed English and got the help he required from literally the girl next door.

Ruta "Ruth" Taylor was a stocky and smart Slavic girl, an emigre from Lithuania by way of Glasgow, and ten years in America when Abe arrived. She taught him the language and the ropes, and they would make a life together for nearly sixty years. Their business was Barron's, a notorious and beloved kosher delicatessen on Roosevelt Road about three miles west of the Chicago Maternity Center. In the 20s and 30s it was *the* socialist hangout on the old West Side—corned beef on rye, chocolate phosphates and revolutionary commiseration. Emma Goldman ate there once. And Saul Alinsky, destined for fame as a laborite and community organizer, was in those days just another one of the University of Chicago boys who'd sit there for hours nursing "a glass tea," talking their radical politics. Abe called them the gradual students.

Nick's mother was Abe and Ruth's youngest child. They named her Thalia, after a comedic and beautiful Greek muse, and for her entire life everyone called her Tally. Tally Barron was, in the neighborhood vernacular, a *shayna maideleh*, a dark-eyed, dark-skinned knockout who was the family darling, the sweetheart of the deli, and the object of crush upon crush from kindergarten to college. She was smart and modern enough to study journalism at Northwestern University in Evanston, and then smitten enough to give up school and a career for Jacob "Jack" Weissman, a handsome and streetwise charmer who'd been pursuing her since high school.

Though in her parents' minds there was likely not a man in all of Chicago good enough for Tally, Abe and Ruth were particularly aggrieved at her choice of this young man. Jack was the son of shtetl Jews, a Polish junk man and his babushka, uneducated, unsophisticated, a family they considered unworthy of their bright and beautiful daughter. And roots aside, they weren't fond of Jack himself. They thought he was a brash opportunist, a lady's man whose swagger and good looks and sharp clothes had swept their daughter off her feet, and who would surely disappoint her. Tally, the modern girl, would have none of their protestations.

Tally and Jack married in 1937 and by their second anniversary Nick's big sister Natalie was three months old. Jack was selling wholesale cleaning products for the Johnson's Wax Company, making just enough money for food and shelter in their tiny apartment in Douglas Park. By the time Nick came along in the winter of 1944, Jack had gone through three more jobs, had no savings and no prospects. With the deli flourishing, Abe and Ruth decided that Tally's circumstances were unacceptable and that they could afford to do something about it. Abe was not surprised when Jack, whom he considered a *schnorer*, a pretentious sponger, accepted his offer after a moment's display of prideful resistance. Abe would supplement Jack's income so that the young family could move into a larger apartment and hire a "girl" to come in five days a week to clean, cook and help with the children. This was *de rigeur* for a respectable West Side Jewish household and Tally deserved no less. For Tally's long-term security, Abe would lend Jack enough money to establish his own business subject to Abe's approval.

After Nick—"Nicky" for most of his childhood—was born, they moved to a three bedroom apartment on Congress Street in Garfield Park. This was a fine upgrade, but would serve them for only seven years. Shortly after the move, Jack, in partnership with his cousin Lenny and with Abe's money and guidance, took over a downtown restaurant. They renamed it Pierre's—they thought it sounded classy—and made a go of it. Lenny was a responsible young man who diligently tended to detail, and Jack was perfectly suited for schmoozing the customers. With Abe's patronage and Lenny's reliability, Jack had found a sweet spot, a good living where he could be himself, the amiable kibitzer.

In 1951, second-grader Nicky was seven years old, Pierre's was going strong, and Jack and Tally were talking almost every day about leaving the West Side. The Congress Street Expressway—later called the Eisenhower—would begin construction in 1953. Their apartment building would remain standing but they would live next to a construction zone for at least two years and then have to abide the sight, the noise and the smell of an interstate highway permanently. They knew they needed to relocate somewhere, but their desire to abandon the West Side entirely had nothing to do with highway construction. With Blacks flooding into the inner-city by the hundreds of thousands, the Weissman's next move was an uncamouflaged and unapologetic racial evacuation.

Just in time for Nicky to start third grade in his new school, Jack and Tally brought the family to West Rogers Park, an all-white, nearly all-Jewish middle class neighborhood at the north end of the city. Abe and Ruth would follow a year later. There were no phony justifications or hollow rationalizations for the moves. It was plainly stated and repeated that "we should be with our own."

In their new surroundings, Jack and Tally worried about their children about as much as the other parents in West Rogers Park, which meant that they worried about them every waking moment. The "be carefuls" were relentless—about crossing the street, about roughhousing, about going out with a wet head, about swimming after eating, about strangers, about being out after dark, about sitting too close to the newly acquired television set, about, well, life itself. It didn't help that a month after they arrived a neighbor boy, a year older than Nicky, was struck and killed by a car in front of their apartment building. They'd surrounded themselves with Jews and kept the Blacks a half a city away, and still the world was dangerous. Fear and caution were endemic, woven into the fabric of their everyday life. It was 1951, a mere six years after the liberation of Auschwitz and Buchenwald.

The Weissman's Jewishness was tightly bound to kinship, familiarity and security, less to the synagogue than to homogeneity and its promise of safety. Nick would attend Hebrew School and read from the scrolls at his Bar

Mitzvah, not so much as an expression of piety or any meaningful Weissman tradition of worship, but as a fulfillment of social expectation, a *nachas*-generating rite of passage that was mandatory as a matter of tribal identity. In this second-generation Jewish-American family, and many like it, God was not conspicuously in the equation.

Elementary and high school for Nick were academically easy and socially awkward. He was small, looking up at many of the girls until well into tenth grade, self-conscious about his skin, as olive as ever and acne-ridden for most of his adolescence, and not in the circle of the cooler kids. He was occasionally bullied, but his intelligence and the conditioned caution of his upbringing reliably kept him out of harm's way in seventh and eighth grades and in high school. His claim to fame, or at least to avoidance of the desolation of the completely uncool, was his drumming.

He played in his high school concert and marching bands, in a jazz trio, and most passionately in a rock and roll band that included two prodigies who were miles ahead of Nick and the others musically. Still, it was unimaginable that the two of them were about to break through the stratosphere of their musical world. In 1965, only four years out of high school, they would be on stage with Bob Dylan when he famously "went electric" at the Newport Folk Festival.

While Nick would not regret the path that lay ahead—premed, med school and doctorhood—his brush with rock and roll greatness would for years fuel his fantasies, the what-ifs of his own imagined musical journey, and his mixture of envy and vicarious pleasure at the triumph of his bandmates.

Nick's decision for a career in medicine was made with little conflict. He would be the first doctor in the family, honorable and honored. He would assure financial success and security, and he would avoid, or so he thought, the aggravations of his father's world of business. He would be "in service," which appealed, and he was confident that he was smart enough to make it through the academic gauntlet.

As a pre-med at the University of Illinois in Champaign-Urbana he quickly learned that desire and discipline were at least as important as intelligence for the competitive battle for medical school admission. The hours, the cramming, the Dexedrine-caffeine all-nighters were mostly exercises in memorization. Brainbusters like organic chemistry demanded complex problem-solving and visualization of molecular structures in three dimensional space (Nick never would get a handle on these), but more typically the task was committing to memory the hundreds of Latinate names of arteries, veins, muscles and nerves—of a cat. If he could retain the preposterous gaggle of information required for each test, then he would survive.

The attributes of judgment, of empathy, of integrity, of common sense, were neither mentioned nor measured as criteria for his admission to medical school—and admission to medical school put him on the two yard line for becoming a physician. He understood that the rate-limiting step to a medical career had been the pre-med scrum, the four years of competitive grinding with more losers than winners in the end. Once he was admitted to med school, despite the physical and intellectual demands, it was a downhill journey to his M.D.

The Street

The word on Ernie Johnson was that he'd been to prison. For what, no one knew, and no one was asking. His official title at the Maternity Center was Custodian, though he'd long since left janitorial labor behind. A real job description would have included at least historian, counselor, tour guide and guardian angel of the physical premises and its very white medical students. Ernie was, first of all, huge—at least six five, maybe two eighty. He wore tight black t-shirts, showing off his enormous biceps and less flatteringly a massive overhanging gut. Blacker than most black men, he sported a shaven head and a pirate smile, incandescent featuring one gold central incisor. Ernie stories abounded, from surprise midnight pizza deliveries at the barracks to whorehouse escorts for the least varnished of medical students. It was told and retold that he'd thrown an intruder out a third story window at the Center after discovering him pawing one of the nursing students. Supposedly killed him.

Ernie showed up at the barracks on day three asking if anyone wanted to see Maxwell Street. It was a cold but clear afternoon, and Nick and Jeff, last and next to last up for deliveries, jumped at the prospect of a few hours out in the world. They were barely into their Maternity Center fortnight but it already felt like a siege. The Center, the slum tenements, the barracks, the bleak and scary territory of the West Side ghetto, had that quickly saturated their senses and depleted their confidence, their fragile medical student grip on their trial-by-fire universe. They didn't say it aloud, but they were, to a man, afraid. Nick spent his solitary hours immersed in worst case scenarios, from dead mothers and babies to mugged and mutilated doctors-to-be. A respite of fresh air and sunshine on Maxwell Street was welcome.

Nick's most vivid Maxwell memories were of the street musicians, the Mississippi Delta bluesmen who played for coins tossed by the shoppers and the standarounds. On weekends Nick and his high school bandmates would come down from the North Side to hear the blues, the live unadulterated sidewalk blues that you couldn't hear on vinyl or even in the clubs. But Nick's earliest memory of the Street was something else—shopping with his father for a bargain of a bar mitzvah suit. They went first to Irv Benjamin's and then to the classier Gabel's, where his dad bought him a sharp three button, black pinstripes on gray worsted. In a framed photo on his mother's dresser, it still looked sharp.

The three of them, Ernie and Jeff and Nick, walked the five minutes from the barracks to the heart of the street market, the intersection of Maxwell and Halsted. Nick could smell it before he saw it, the sweet aura of onions emanating from Jimmy's, the big hot dog stand on the main corner. It seemed like you could get a Vienna red hot on just about any commercial block in this city, but Jimmy's was *the* place on Maxwell, the overwhelming favorite. Nick ordered two Chicago koshers exactly the way he'd had them for as long as he could remember—boiled dogs on poppy seed buns from a steamer, bright yellow mustard, neon green relish, chopped raw onion, thin slivers of tomato, a quarter of a dill pickle, all of it sprinkled with celery salt. Nick's New York cousins, devotees of Nathan's and sauerkraut, considered the Chicago version perverse, and the contempt, wienerwise, was reciprocated. They could all agree, though, that ketchup on a kosher hot dog was an abomination.

Nick and Jeff strolled out onto Maxwell with Ernie trailing as he was glad-handed and back-slapped along the way, the big man an obvious favorite of the curbside vendors. Heading east, Nick ate his properly accessorized Viennas as he walked, gratified with the texture and taste of this very specific Chicago pleasure, a small but perfect fulfillment of expectation. He was less pleased, though, with the street market itself, an unexpectation, a dull surprise of a kind that as he grew older was becoming familiar. He'd brought to the moment the visual and tactile and olfactory certainties of personal history, of lifelong experience, and their instant evaporation left him not just uncertain about his memories, but sad. He felt quite like this only a few seasons earlier, exploring another tributary of his past.

He'd gone the previous August to re-visit the summer

place of his childhood, a house on Lake Michigan's shore in Miller Beach, Indiana. For eight years his extended family, ten of them including Grandpa Abe and Grandma Ruth, stayed from the Fourth of July to Labor Day in a rented home at the water's edge. Nick and his sister and two first cousins had the entire basement to themselves, where they slept and played and kept their clothes and toys. This lower level was happily off-limits to the adults, who referred to it, not ironically, as Camp Slob. The more orderly (cleaner, that is, not by any means quieter) main floor of the house was basically adult territory. Except for meals, Nick and the other kids were either in the basement, the grassy front yard or out back on the beach. They played and played and ate and slept and took entirely for granted, as they should have, that they were loved and safe in this family and in this special place. It was communal, each of the half dozen adults looking after the four kids and the household chores, and it was boisterous (to be kind), the adults arguing among themselves and criticizing and gossiping, giving unsolicited advice on every imaginable subject, the talking outweighing the listening by a landslide.

Returning to the beach house after a thirteen year absence, Nick thought he'd gone to the wrong address. Could this tiny cottage possibly be the place he remembered? Camp Slob, cavernous he'd thought, was claustrophobic, the wonderful front lawn a puny patch, the spacious main floor a warren of little boxes with low oppressive ceilings, the big beach a narrow strip of sand and stones. Was it simply the imprinting of his child's-eye view that was the substrate for his disappointment, or was it something more? Had he over the years embellished this childhood place, idealized it, reconstructed his recollection to enrich it, enlarge it, give it more gravity? He sat in the cottage's tiny kitchen questioning his reality—how much did he bend the past to his liking? How much did everyone?

Maxwell Street on this Tuesday afternoon was another betrayal of coveted memory. Nick's Maxwell Street Market was a four block pedestrian ocean of bargain hunters and pitchmen, tables and stalls and pushcarts piled high with every imaginable household good and garment, the din of thousands of hagglers in cacophony with curbside amplifiers emitting harmonica and electric guitar and delta poetry, the smell of those onions and cooked meats and urine and sweat and fresh fruit and flowers and rotting garbage. You could hear Yiddish and Polish and Spanish and several varieties of English. There were "pullers" in the doorways, the men who used whatever the law allowed (and sometimes more) to get passersby into the shops, and there was an ever-present old bluesman with a live chicken on his head.

Today the scene was skeletal, not barren but not remotely bustling. The hawkers' tables were a scattered array punctuated by yards of unused sidewalk. Shoppers, mostly in ones and twos, meandered amid the merchandise with plenty of elbow room and an unfrenzied pace. The prevailing sound was not the music of agitated negotiation or amplified blues. It was instead the whistling and wailing of the Hawk, the local name for the razor wind blowing cold across Chicago from the Great Lakes. The doorways to the permanent storefronts, unlocked but closed against the weather, were mostly undisturbed. Minutes earlier Nick had hyped the Maxwell Street Market to Jeff, who'd never been there, telling him how amazing it was, what a mob scene it was. Now he felt foolish. "Well," he said, "it used to be amazing. Maybe it still is on the weekends."

Crossing Jefferson Street, once the heart of the market, Nick got a small dose of vindication at the sight of a blues trio playing on the sidewalk about fifty yards to their right. He and Jeff headed down the empty street toward the little combo, a woman in a wheelchair tapping a tambourine, a man standing with an electric guitar, and a second man with a harmonica in one hand and a microphone in the other. They were all three in overcoats, both men donning the essential blues hat, a dark felt fedora, and the woman wearing something like an Easter bonnet, a bright white wide-brim with a cluster of fake flowers. Off the beaten path and with no obvious receptacle for tips—no glass jar or open guitar case—they were playing for themselves, for the pleasure of it. Nick didn't recognize the particular tune but the form was embedded in his drummer soul. Twelve bar blues, the three chord bone marrow of this music and its rock and roll progeny. The woman tapped the tambourine on the back beat, the two and four of each measure, and took turns with the guitar player on the vocals. The harmonica player filled with whoops and wails between the lines and traded solos with the guitar.

Nick and Jeff watched and listened from a respectful distance, twenty feet or so. The trio finished what they were playing and Nick knew the next song as soon as they started, though it began with an inside verse:

Now if the river was whiskey
And I was a divin' duck

This was *Rollin' and Tumblin'*, the Muddy Waters chestnut that Nick had known for years. These people did it slow, slower than he'd ever heard it played, and stretched it out with a harmonica and a guitar cycle between every verse.

Well I could a had a religion
This bad old thing instead

Nick knew that these three were the real deal, from the same Delta DNA as Robert Johnson and Leadbelly, Mississippi John Hurt and Willie Dixon. The guitarist was playing slide, his left little finger encased in glass fashioned from the neck of a beer bottle. The harmonica man used a microphone shaped like a fat blunt bullet, the amplified weapon of choice for any respectable Chicago harp player.

Well, I rolled and I tumbled
Cried the whole night long

Nick thought it odd that all three musicians now seemed to be looking directly at him as they played, and then realized that they were looking not at him but just past him, at something or someone behind him. He turned around and there was a moment of nothing, of complete loss of the prior moment and paralysis in the next, and in that insentient instant his brain stem and adrenal glands, his body's unconscious emergency center that had evolved for hundreds of thousands of years for moments like these, did what it was supposed to do. Before his "I'm screwed" conversation with himself could even begin, his sympathetic nervous system was in overdrive, adrenaline escalating his heart rate and respirations, pupils dilating, blood flooding to his arms and legs. Sudden fear does this. The biologic response to immediate danger, the readiness for extreme action, this was "fight or flight," and Nick was in no position for either.

He faced three young men standing no more than two feet from him. They each wore a black leather coat, knee length with wide pointed lapels and an ornate patch over the left breast pocket. He would soon enough know its meaning. Two of them donned fedoras and the third had an uncovered and untamed afro with a long-handled hair pick lodged above his right ear. The tallest of the three, fedoraed with a beard and sunglasses and arms folded across his chest, spoke like he owned the sidewalk. "You like the blues, do ya?" This caused Jeff to turn around and join his fellow medical student in dreadful attention.

Nick stood perfectly still, avoiding eye contact with any of them. His thoughts careened while the threat inhabited his body—his throat, chest, gut, armpits. *Don't look at them...don't argue...don't freak out.*

"I asked you if you like the blues."

"Look," Nick said almost inaudibly, "we don't want any trouble."

"What'd you say?"

"I just said we don't want any trouble." He said it about ten decibels louder, his eyes on the man's torso.

"Trouble? What kinda trouble you talkin' about?" Meting out the intimidation in increments, he leaned toward Nick waiting for an answer.

The musicians were still playing and Nick, starting to regain his wits if not his nerve, felt a measure of safety in their presence. "Look, we're here to deliver babies. We're medical students working over at the Maternity Center on Newberry."

They'd been told at orientation that the medical student rotation was basically safe, which Nick thought was the sort of thing you say when something was not really safe. Doctor Butler said that the neighborhood gave the students and nurses a wide berth because they knew they were doing good works. But Bobby Plunkett was robbed on day one, and here he and Jeff were, scared clueless about what was going to happen next.

The tall one pressed in well past civil distance, inches from Nick. "So you're here to practice on our sisters, is that it?"

Nick knew that that was exactly what he and Jeff and the others were there to do, but this was hardly a moment for transparency or a nuanced discussion of the ethics of medical education in the inner-city. It wasn't, anyway, a question. It was sadism, a small turn of the screw to frighten and humiliate. Still, he answered. As long as they were talking, no matter the disingenuousness of the dialogue, at least he wasn't being punched, kicked, stabbed or shot, all of which seemed shockingly possible. "Look, we're just here to try to help."

The tall one arched his eyebrows and spoke through a minstrel grin. "So you white boys gonna help us po' black folk, huh?" When the young man's cool countenance returned, Nick saw that the muscles over his jaws were bulging, then relaxing, then bulging again, as though he were grinding his teeth. Nick thought him even more dangerous than moments before—coiled. Then Jeff decided to negotiate.

"Here," Jeff said. "Here's my money. Will you please just take it and go?" His right arm was fully extended with a small wad of folded bills between his thumb and index finger. The tall man uncoiled, his right hand driving upward through Jeff's, the bills scattering like butterflies.

"You think we want your fuckin' money? You think that's what we want?"

Nick took a step back and bumped into the man with the hair pick, who had circled behind and now shoved him, hard, toward the tall one who grabbed him by the collar with both hands. He could feel his heart slamming against his breast bone, and at some point amid these scary seconds the music stopped. Like an animal in submission, which indeed he was, he kept his eyes down, staring at the patch on the man's leather coat. It was some kind of symbol, a horizontal mirror image with concentric circles and finger-like projections. For several seconds, there was the intimidation of silence and the man's hands pressing into his neck, of nothing but peril. And then something changed. It was subtle but unequivocal, a shift in the man's posture, a slight backing away, then a footfall from behind. When the grip on his collar loosened, Nick was certain his luck had changed. His first thought, and desperate hope, was that it was the local cops. He was wrong.

Ernie followed a basic law of the street: when outnumbered, you pick out the leader and humiliate him in front of his followers. Nick was knocked aside as collateral damage while the full force of the collision exploded into the tall man. Like a linebacker from hell, Ernie and his two hundred and eighty pounds hit him square on at full speed, propelling him fifteen feet backwards and flat on his back. Ernie grabbed him by the collar with both hands and lifted him to his feet.

"How does that feel?" Ernie said. "How do you like it?"

"Hey old man, this ain't none of your business."

"Now you listen to me," Ernie said, "these boys are my business. You do yourself a big favor, boy, and walk away. You and your friends just walk away, right now." Ernie's size and command had instantly and utterly shifted the balance of power. The tall one kept talking but Nick could see that he was on his heels, attitude up front but backing away slowly, trying to save face and his own skin at the same time.

"You better be careful around here, old man. You better watch yourself."

"Yeah, yeah, you and your friends just get outta here," Ernie said, glaring the three of them into submission.

They walked down Jefferson Street, at a pace so intentionally slow that it could not be taken as anything other than defiance. When they were about thirty yards away the tall one turned and yelled, "We'll be lookin' for ya, old man. We'll be lookin'." Then the three of them began talking and laughing. A little too loudly, Nick thought.

"They're Abrafo," Ernie said. "Blue Island Abrafo."

They were in a booth at La Taqueria on Halsted Street off Maxwell, Nick and Jeff side by side opposite Ernie. Nick rearranged the rice on a tamale combo, his white plastic fork transmitting a visible tremor. They'd been out of harm's way for almost a half an hour but his nervous system was still abuzz—hands shaking, vigilant, faintly nauseous. The tamales were probably a mistake.

Jeff asked Ernie for a translation of Abrafo. "It means executioner in some kinda African," Ernie said, and went on to tell them about the least known and scariest street gang on the Near West Side. "Even the Lords and the Rangers don't come down here and mess with 'em." He was talking about the Vice Lords and the Blackstone Rangers, Chicago's largest and most notorious black street gangs. "Started by a bunch of ex-Lords livin' 'round Blue Island Avenue, thought the Lords were goin' soft, turnin' to community service and all that. The Abrafo are hoodlums, straight up, collectin' protection money from the shopkeepers, trashin' their places and beatin' 'em up if they don't pay. Just like the Italians, but less to lose and that makes 'em even more dangerous. And they're stupid, man they're stupid, gettin' into it with you white boys. See, the cops don't give a shit about Black on Black, one brother beatin' on another brother, they could care less. But beat up a white boy and they'll send out half the fuckin' black and whites in the precinct. You just don't do it, man. But these Abrafo, some of 'em anyway, they're just fuckin' stupid."

Jeff asked about the patches on their coats. Ernie said the Abrafo always had that symbol somewhere on their clothing, and that some of them had it tattooed, usually on their arms. "It's supposed to be the sign of some African warrior."

Nick meanwhile was busy thinking that stupid and violent was not a good combination. And right behind that he was thinking that he wanted to quit and go home to the safety of West Rogers Park. Was there anything in this place that was worth risking limb or life? Had he, a rank amateur, somehow become obstetrically indispensable? Would these experiences matter in the least in his life as a physician? Fresh in the throes of fear, the case was lopsided. It was insane to be in this place—undertrained, at times unsupervised, and of utmost concern at the moment, endangered.

Late that night, though, in the dark and quiet place before sleep, in the permeable realm of undefended thoughts and unwelcome truths, he navigated the landscape of his own culpability. He'd said to himself that Bobby Plunkett was "breathtakingly stupid" to be walking alone in this neighborhood, yet he and Jeff had wandered down a deserted street save three septuagenarian musicians. Perhaps not breathtaking, but certainly stupid. And what had actually happened at the hands of the Abrafo? He was not punched, kicked, stabbed or shot. He wasn't even robbed. Christ, Plunkett was robbed with a gun in his ribs and he didn't freak out. Yeah, maybe something else might have happened had Ernie not come along, but maybe nothing else would have happened, perhaps there would have been nothing more than intimidation, schoolyard bullying. In considering his immediate future, Nick could make a case for being sensibly cautious, but he could also, in the cover of darkness, make a case for his own cowardice. And what would his responses have been if the three young men had been white? Would there have been the same measure of fear at first sight? Would the entire incident have had less power? Was he not, despite his liberal politics and his contempt for his father's *schvartze*-laden vocabulary and his love of the blues, fearful of young black men? To what extent was his urge to quit realistic, and to what extent was it, oh Jesus, racist.

His dead of night was ruthless, a shadowland populated by doubt and self-recrimination. The light of day would disinfect, but Nick Weissman fell asleep a bigot and a coward.

The Promise

"Mom, you worry too much."

It was Nick's first telephone call from the Maternity Center to his mother, who was none too happy about her son's ghetto adventure. The probability that he was going to tell her about his encounter with the Abrafo was, well, zero. He'd never been forthcoming with his parents about anything that would raise concern about his well-being, particularly his safety. His big sister Natalie was, unlike him, a daily caller and a sieve when it came to filtering information, regardless of the amount of anxiety it provoked. As a teenager, she'd kept the household in a state of routine agitation. This only reinforced Nick's inclination to keep his mouth shut and his parents' belief that he rarely got into trouble. They did, however, consider him a lousy correspondent.

"I worry too much?" his mother said. "You're out day and night in the worst neighborhoods in Chicago and I worry too much?"

"Mom, I'm all right, really."

"We can't know that if you don't call us. It's been six days."

"I just called. This is a call, mom. We're having a call."

"All right, don't be such a wise guy. Could you just this once stay in touch? We worry about you."

He'd worked it out that if he called frequently, say once a day, it would be so out of character that his parents would worry more, that only something really worrisome would lead him, the lousy correspondent, to reliably correspond. He was, he could argue, protecting them, being considerate. On the other hand, he could argue, to himself anyway and more persuasively, that he was full of shit. In the eight years that he'd been out of the house—four years at college and four in medical school—he'd kept his parents at arm's length because that's the way he wanted it. While his distance was hardly unique—go have sons—it was tenaciously maintained, as though his separateness were a fragile thing. He could be forthcoming and accept all manner of advice from friends and classmates, but parents were another matter. He did not want to hear from them that he should study hard or eat better or dress warmer, or that it would be wonderful if he met somebody. Thing is, though, Tally Weissman rarely said such things and his father, as far as he could tell, did not even think them. While the stereotype of the Jewish mother was readily available and darkly enjoyable to inflict, his mother was in fact not a noodge, a pest, a hovering smothering maternal presence, and he knew it.

"Look, I'm sorry," he said. "I'll check in every couple

days, okay?"

His intention was precisely that. His information would be filtered, sanitized of anything provocative, anything that would stir the pot of inner-city fear and trembling, hers or his own. He would assure her, every other day, that all was well.

The Maternity Center Clinic, eight steps down from street level, exuded all the ambience and charm of a bus station. Its waiting area was dimly illuminated through narrow transoms, Chicago's winter sky a reliable source of gray which decolorized everything it touched. The floor, a barber shop mosaic of small white hexagonal tiles, held the season's chill in its ceramic grip. Its antidotes were steam heat from uncovered radiators lining three of the four walls, and an arrangement of two sets of double doors at the entry preventing the icy Hawk wind from invading each time somebody came or went. Every available square foot of the waiting area was filled with long dark wooden benches with upright backs which felt as uncomfortable as they looked, and which were occupied to capacity or beyond most of the time. The fourth wall, the one without the radiators, had three square cut openings for contact between the public and the receptionists who, bakery-style, summoned patients by the numbers. Pregnant young women, their abdomens bulging, were crammed side by side on the benches or upright against the walls, while their toddlers and preschoolers, a restless hive of commotion and winter mucus, played amid their feet.

Nick made his way through the crowd as they waited for the morning prenatal clinic to begin. A year earlier he'd spent a month in the private office suites of the Miracle Mile obstetricians, the North Michigan Avenue docs who cared for and delivered the wealthiest women in town. Those waiting rooms were parlors, upholstered sitting rooms with art and music and soft lighting, plush carpet, chairs and sofas that luxuriously accommodated the ever widening rear ends of the pregnant elite of Chicago. Graciously welcomed, those patients were seen of course by appointment, well-spaced and punctual. Barring the unexpected, there was very little waiting in those elegant waiting rooms. Three miles away, the Chicago Maternity Center was a world apart. To Nick the scene was indistinguishable from every public clinic he'd worked in—poor people, overwhelmingly black and brown, crowded and anonymous, waiting for hours to see doctors, or doctors-in-training like him, that they seldom knew. True, it was preferable to the clinic waiting room at Cook County Hospital, where you could not just figuratively die waiting to be seen.

Nick stepped over and around the siblings of the yet-to-be-born, past the receptionist wall, and into a cluster of examination rooms, nursing areas and charting cubicles. He'd shown up following a simple rule for the medical students—if you weren't out doing a delivery or sleeping off a middle-of-the-night case, you came to clinic and saw patients.

Bobby Plunkett was already there and so was Mary the midwife, who was functioning as head nurse. "Heard you had a brush with the Abrafo," she said, taking the measure of Nick's anxiety. In their long hours together at the Helen Jackson delivery, he and Mary had traversed the territory between courteous professionalism and budding friendship, relaxing their defenses and sharing slices of their lives.

Ten years his senior, Mary Williams was a ghetto girl who had made it out with the help of her grandmother, a fierce Baptist church lady who ran out of patience with the drunken neglect of her granddaughter. She took Mary in at age four and spent much of her hard-won savings on parochial elementary and high school tuitions and the cost of Mary's nursing education at Loyola. For years the roles had been reversed, with Mary supporting and caring for her elderly angel. She died the year before Nick arrived at the Center. Mary could be fierce like her grandma, intimidating to Nick at first, but softening with acquaintance.

"Yeah, I guess you could call it a brush," he said. "It was mostly grabbing and shoving, but I don't know what would've happened if Ernie hadn't come along."

"Probably nothing," she said, "but some of those boys are just crazy. You don't know what they're gonna do."

"Thanks for the reassurance."

"Any time, doctor." There it was again, the ironic honorific, served up with something that felt like affection but a reminder still of who Nick was and was not. When a nurse or a real M.D.—a resident or an attending physician—called a medical student *doctor* in front of a patient, that was a bona fide courtesy. When they did it among themselves, it was a kind of hazing, a gentle or not so gentle reminder of professional position. Specifically, one's hind titness.

The clinic was filling up. Larry Berlin walked in with

the obstetrics resident Bill Wong, a likeable. The St. Olaf's nursing students, button-cute in their starchy caps and pink and white striped blouses, escorted the pregnant patients to the exam rooms, and Mary handed out the charts, one each for starters, to the three medical students. Nick kept his discomfort to himself when he saw that his day would begin with Blossom Amos, a fourteen year-old they'd all heard about, laden with twins and nearly mute with depression. He wanted a simple morning, a routine morning, and he was not going to get it. It could not have been a random assignment, he thought, but a reckoning with Mary would have to wait. Stepping into the examination room, he worried about things immediate and tangible: a decent history and physical, a good write-up, pleasing the resident. He knew this teenager was going to be a challenge, as much to his green bedside manner as to his limited skills as a pelvic diagnostician. And he knew that every medical student who had preceded him had failed to connect with this unhappy girl. What Nick could not know was that he was embarking in that moment on the most perilous journey of his young life, wading into a stream which would be joined by unimaginable currents propelling him to the limits of his integrity and courage.

"Good Morning, Miss Amos," he said, expecting no response and getting none. Against a barely chromatic backdrop of gray walls and linoleum, Blossom Amos sat slouched on the side of an examination table, her white stocking feet dangling a foot above the floor. She wore the universally embarrassing patient frock, a faded and shapeless string-tied wraparound, the kind that threatens at any moment to emancipate a normally well concealed body part. Nick thought she looked young for fourteen, her school-age face in stark counterpoint to nearly nine months worth of breasts and belly. There was no drama in her expression, no palpable sadness or fear, no telltales at the corners of her mouth, her eyes, in the soft creases between. She was empty, he thought, another Helen Jackson, another joyless multiparous journey begun.

He'd walked in with something close to foreboding, at a loss for how to communicate with Blossom and a wish for little more than brevity, to do a decent obstetrical evaluation and move on to the next patient. He had no conscious intention of winning her over, and certainly no desire to somehow make himself indispensable in her eyes. Yet despite his inexperience and insecurity and barely camouflaged reticence, he was about to become the object of this girl's affection and trust.

It was, in a way, an accident. Out of simple courtesy, and happy to divert from Blossom's wall of silence, he turned to the woman who had accompanied her to the exam room and introduced himself. Sitting on a metal chair next to the exam table, she spoke through an easy smile. "Hello, I'm Blossom's sister Caroline. She's livin' with us for the time being." He was struck by their resemblance, though Caroline's face revealed the wear and tear of an adult life. He would have readily believed that she was Blossom's mother. Her demeanor was warm and invitational, not sexual but friendly and forthcoming. He was happy to continue his diversion and asked about the us she had mentioned. "It's just me and my two boys," she said. "And Blossom now, and pretty soon her babies." With that, her smile widened, her eyes joining in.

"How old are your sons?" he asked. Without forethought he had placed himself perfectly in relation to Blossom and Caroline, seated on a rolling stool at the point of a triangle that allowed him to speak to either sister while still facing both. Blossom remained inert, slouched, perhaps listening. He couldn't tell.

"Charles is seven," Caroline said, "and Richard is four."

"Would you tell me a little about them?"

"Well, they're good boys. They get in trouble but not big trouble. Richard'll be in kindergarten next year. He's my pistol, can't stop talkin' for a minute. But he's a good boy."

"And Charles?" Nick asked, still stalling.

"He's the quiet one, always has been. Smart too. He'll be finishin' second grade and his teacher says they might skip him, you know move him ahead 'cause he's smarter than the other kids. I don't know if it's a good idea."

"Tell him about Richie." It was Blossom, hardly full-throated but loud enough to be understood. Nick was relieved—at least she said something.

"We're not here for Richie," Caroline said. "We're here for your checkup."

"Damn it," Blossom shouted, "I want you to tell him about Richie!"

Blossom's abrupt agitation was unnerving. At the same time Nick was pleased at his perceived importance, that he must hear the information about Richie, whatever it was. And given his unease with her exam, it was a welcome detour. "It's okay," he said, "tell me about him."

"Well, all right," Caroline said. "They say he's got these spasms, infant spasms. It started when he was about six months and it's still goin' on."

He listened carefully to the description of how Richie would suddenly stare into space and repeatedly jerk his head forward, as though bowing, and of the Cook County doctors' tests and explanations and drugs. Caroline didn't use the word epilepsy, but that was surely a knowing omission. It was unlike Nick to immediately grasp the uncommon, the esoteric, the domain of the specialist, but in this instance he was, improbably, a bit of an expert.

Northwestern's child neurology research center was oddly enough at the local VA Hospital. It was the summer of '63 and Nick at nineteen was working as a lab assistant for an MD, PhD go-getter doing epilepsy research on cats. It didn't pay much but it would be a solid extracurricular asset on his medical school applications. The laboratory work, while scientifically sound, was creepy and at times barbaric. The studies required continuous monitoring of brain waves—EEG's—so these cats had electrodes surgically attached to their shaven skulls. At the end of the experiments, they were sacrificed by intravenous injection and their brains were biopsied. But that wasn't the worst part. The worst part was how the cats were physically restrained in preparation for any of this—asphyxiated to unconsciousness by a wire noose at the end of a long metal pole which kept the handler at a safe distance from flailing claws and threatening teeth. Nick was spared this grizzly task, but he watched without objection, shocked at first but in short order inured. In time his complicity would be a source of shame, the details of the brutal feline goings-on unmentionable, but at nineteen his eyes were on the prize: medical school. It's not that he struggled with the moral dilemma and came down on the side of the researchers. Awash in his quest for approval, he didn't struggle at all.

There was a good part to the job. Three times a week Nick got to go to the neurology clinic at Children's Hospital. All summer long he was a fly on the wall for examinations and discussions of actual human patients, in this case mostly kids with epilepsy. He saw everything, from garden variety to exotic, was privy to the professors' musings, and read voraciously. Among the exotic was a condition called Infantile Spasms, with strange physical manifestations, a unique diagnostic finding on EEG, and a troubled track record in terms of treatment. For two months he followed a little girl with the diagnosis and even got to see a seizure episode in the clinic. He was surprised by its subtlety, which he thought could have been easily mistaken for random movements or some kind of tic. At three this one had no evidence of retardation, but he knew that put her in a small and lucky minority.

He waded in with Caroline. It was as much a chance for him to flex his medical muscles as it was a response to Blossom's angry demand for attention to her nephew. He knew this diagnosis, its variants and treatments and complications. He had something to offer. He began with Richie's development. "Do you remember how old he was when he was first able to sit up by himself?" Then he asked about crawling and standing and walking. Then about his speech and toilet training. Nick was unplanfully fluent, at ease, his med student anxiety and self-consciousness giving way to the competence of the moment. He'd had breakthroughs like this before, and it would be their accumulation, not degrees or licenses, that would soon enough seal his identity as *physician.*

Blossom was out of her slouch now, attentive, hanging on to everything that Nick asked and Caroline answered. After going through Richie's development, he inventoried his behavior, the details of his seizures, the effects, good and bad, of his medications. It seemed that the Cook County doctors were on top of it, that the diagnostic studies and the drugs prescribed were appropriate. Still, Richie's spasms continued and the prognosis, he knew, was terrible. He felt the pressure to offer something, anything that might be helpful. He'd encouraged the discussion, flashed his un-common knowledge, and now was feeling the weight of the family's desperation. He'd confidently, vainly, played doctor—the thing that you do until you are one—and now he faced their hopeful silence and his own limitations. The sisters watched and waited as though he were a Samaritan, some kind of blessed messenger, a person whose next words would make a difference. Their expectancy filled the color-less room and held him hostage to possibility. He was out of his depth, not about Richie's condition but as a vessel of empathy, a seasoned healer's voice that could transmit disappointment with grace. Finally he relieved himself with the only thing that he could think of.

"Look," he said, "I know the Chief of Pediatric Neurology at Children's Hospital. I can't promise, but I think I could get him to see Richie. There's probably no one better in the city." It was at once an evasion and a gift, and it was received as the latter. Caroline rose to thank him, and as he stood in response he saw Blossom's eyes well with tears. Embarrassed, she tipped her head down, the tops of her fists wiping her cheekbones.

"That's so kind of you," Caroline said. "It's been so hard, we never get..."

There were two rapid knocks on the exam room door. It opened without invitation and Bill Wong, the resident, leaned in and asked Nick if he was ready to talk about Blossom. Nick explained the delay, Wong withdrew, and attention by necessity turned to original business. "I'll talk to the Neurology Chief at Children's" Nick said to Blossom, "but we'd better get to you and your twins."

The accident had happened. By way of pride and coincidence he'd made himself an ally of this little family. To his obstetrical questions, Blossom was responsive, even talkative. She relaxed for the pelvic exam, at one point joking about the temperature of the speculum. When he explained that Dr. Wong would have to briefly repeat the examination, her consent was casual. Nick had become the entrusted and there was trust-by-association.

After the exams, he huddled in a charting alcove with Wong and they agreed that with one important exception—both twins were in breech position—Blossom and her babies were doing well. By dates she was starting her ninth month and that was confirmed by physical examination. When Wong asked Nick to sum up, he said that the delivery would be challenging, probably in the hospital, possibly by cesarean section, but at least the newborns would not be premature. "Not probably in the hospital," Wong corrected, "this one we definitely do in the hospital. But let's get her to at least thirty-eight weeks if we can."

"Well, the twins are still headed out feet first," Nick said. He was back in the exam room wrapping up with Blossom and Caroline. The morning clinic was getting behind and he was feeling pressed to move on to the next patient. He shared the plan that Wong had laid out, and in an apologetic pose, his hand over his heart, re-stated the likelihood that Blossom would deliver not at home but in the hospital. The apology was for "the hospital," which meant Cook County Hospital, for locals a dreaded destination. He expected disappointment, maybe resistance or even anger, but got something else entirely—surprising, flattering, and, he thought, a little crazy. Blossom did not care, it turned out, where she delivered. She did care, very much and suddenly, by whom she was delivered.

"I want you to be my doctor," she said. "I want you to deliver my babies." She had stood up and taken a step toward him just before she spoke. He was at least a foot taller and it felt like he was looking straight down into her upturned face. He answered without a kernel of professional élan.

"I can't, I just can't," he said. "I'm a medical student and you're a complicated delivery."

She was crying again, immune to the young man who

had just depersonalized her, interested only in the "doctor" who was willing to help her beloved nephew. "Why not?" she said, her voice quivering. "Medical students from here deliver babies all the time."

He tried again, shaken by her emotion, and this time with a measure of forethought. Instinctively helping himself, he spoke slowly and quietly. "Look, I can see you're upset and I'm sorry. We only want to do what's best for you and your babies. Breech deliveries require skill and experience and so do twin deliveries. Blossom, I'm telling you, believe me, you want the best person possible and that isn't me."

She stood silently for several seconds, turned to Caroline and then back to Nick. "Well, if you can't deliver them," she said, "will you at least promise to be there?"

The space between her question and his answer was the distance from one breath to the next, but he would revisit the moment for years. Considered rationally, Blossom's question did not make the grade, and nor did Nick's answer. Her urgent belief in him as a medical savior of *anybody* was naive and desperate. He had luckily known something about her nephew's uncommon affliction, and he had done nothing more than say he would talk to a senior specialist about it, someone who probably would have little to add to the boy's care. For his part, his split second calculus blithely ignored the part of his brain that dealt with things like calendars, student rotations and basic physics. He would not, for example, be able to be in two places at the same time, no matter the urgency. She'd invented him, competent and reliable, on the spot, and he, a concoction of sweet upbringing and vanity, good intention and anticipatory guilt, could not say no. On balance, he did it out of kindness.

"Okay," he said. "I'll be there when you deliver."

"Do you promise?"

"Yeah, I promise."

Then Blossom, still tearful, hugged him, her twins pressing into his body. He stood, motionless, arms at his sides, waiting for her to let go.

Part Two

Birmingham

As Nick Weissman stood silent in his covenant with Blossom Amos, seven hundred miles to the south a man walked into a sporting goods store in Birmingham, Alabama carrying a Remington bolt-action rifle. He'd been free for eleven months, his journey unique as the only successful escapee in the history of Jeff City, the Missouri State Penitentiary. In his left hand was a GameMaster 760 equipped with a Redfield scope. After a day's reflection, he'd decided that this particular rifle was insufficient for his purpose. The suitably named middle-aged man behind the counter, Robert Gunner, was surprised to see him, and disappointed. Gunner thought he was there to return the rifle and get his money back.

"Hello again, Mister Lowmeyer. What can I do for you, sir?"

The customer used the name Harvey Lowmeyer for the purchase the day before, a departure from Eric Galt, his mainstay alias since prison. But let's call him by his given name. James Earl Ray looked about forty and to an un-discerning eye was well turned out. The slacks of his gray suit were sharply creased but in direct light had the patina of seared polyester. His shoes, phony alligator, were also betrayed by their luster, which looked like it might have come from a spray can. His ebony hair was pomade slick, combed straight back from a high forehead, its darkness in relief against his wan complexion. His was a countenance in harsh black and white.

"This isn't enough gun." Ray said. "My brother tells me it'll be hard to bring down a big buck with a two-forty-three."

Gunner had family in what he liked to call the hick Midwest, Southern Illinois and Missouri, and knew their dialect when he heard it. It was the way they said a word like hard, the *ar* ringing and full in the back of the mouth. Southerners said it soft and breathy. This customer had the red "Heart of Dixie" Alabama plates on his '66 Mustang and said *ah* for I, but he was no son of the deep south.

"Really?" Gunner said. "Folks 'round here take down white tail with their two-forty-three's season after season, no complaint. You want the thirty-aught-six, I'll sell it to you, sir. It'll cost you more and it's more than you need, but I'll be happy to take your money."

Ray asked to see the more powerful Remington, his head turned just enough to miss Gunner's affable gaze. There was nothing unusual in this. Ray rarely looked straight on at anyone. His avoidant blue eyes, shuttered under layered lids, were divided by a long nose whose tip bent to the right.

This was the intended result of a painful self-adjustment after a nose job only weeks earlier, just one twist on his obsession to be unrecognizable. A fugitive from the past and a starkly imagined future, Ray cultivated his anonymity, his forgettableness.

Waiting on him the day before, Gunner thought him an uncomfortable man, fidgety, tugging at his ear, grimacing. Today he was the same, tic-ridden, eyes rapidly blinking, giggling for no apparent reason. But Gunner's appreciation of the man's nervousness was untethered to any judgment about selling him the rifle. It's not that he sized him up, thought about it, and concluded that he was suitable for gun ownership. That consideration was not in play. He was there to sell, to help, but not to judge who should own one. This was gun country, no questions asked. It didn't matter that deer season was six months off and that legal prey in late March was wild turkey, a creature likely vaporized by the man's weapon of choice.

Gunner went into the back room to get a thirty-aught-six, leaving his customer alone in the front of the store. Restless, Ray paced the display racks, his labored steps in counterpoint to his age and lanky frame, the gait of an older and heavier man. He walked among the cleaning kits, the targets, the grips, slings and holsters, and took notice of none of it. His attention was elsewhere. He was single-minded, this new rifle owner, an erstwhile drifter, thief and convict whose life now had the form and force of grand ambition. His odyssey had been a patchwork of criminal opportunism, flight, capture and flight again, a crooked journey through three countries, twenty-seven states and two penitentiaries. Now he was focused.

It was focus that got him out of Jeff City. With seven years served and eighteen to go, his obsession was escape from a place that was considered inescapable. He was smarter than the average convict and by choice barely visible, a nobody, a low-profile loner who served his time and stayed out of trouble. His day job was in the prison bakery, and it was from there that he would make his way to freedom. He planned it meticulously. Through restless nights, buzzed on amphetamines, he conceived it, revised it, rehearsed it on the stage of his fevered imagination. When the day came he was ready. He knew that it was a good plan, that he had a chance.

He'd hoarded his meager prison salary for years, enough to recruit an inmate accomplice and still have three hundred dollars which he stuffed in his shoes on the morning of the escape. His plan was simple—he would go out in the back of a bakery truck, crouched out of sight beneath a foreshortened bread bin. It was a magician's standby, the false bottom. The metal bin, one of dozens in the bakery, was modified inch by inch over weeks and camouflaged amid its stacked counterparts. A few days before the attempt he hid a set of clothing, its prison markings blacked out, behind a cabinet in the bakery break room.

On the morning of April 23, 1967 he ate a huge breakfast, a dozen eggs, and stuffed his pockets with candy bars that he'd been stashing. In the bakery bathroom he stripped off his prison greens, put on his "civilian" shirt and pants, and then his greens back on over them. During the mid-morning rest period, with the bakery crew out of sight in the break room, he climbed into the bottom of the modified bread bin. His helper, a dishwasher, placed the upper compartment above him and filled it with loaves of bread. Then he closed the hinged lid and at the loading dock shoved the bin onto a waiting flatbed along with four others that were destined for the prison honor farm. When the driver reached the main gate, inspection of the bins was a momentary glance beneath barely elevated lids. To be sure that he was out of sight of the guards at the gate, he waited until the truck made its first turn, then swiftly climbed out of the bin and stripped off his prison layer. When the truck slowed for a sharp turn for the honor farm he jumped to the road and scampered into a ditch for cover. He was a free man and would be for the next four hundred and eleven days.

Gunner emerged with a very different rifle. "Here you go, Mister Lowmeyer. This is a pump-action thirty-aught-six, I think you'll like it."

Ray took it by the wood with both hands, the orange-brown walnut flanking the cold metal of the magazine and trigger assemblies. His left hand cradled the forearm, the pump that slid rearward to eject a spent cartridge and forward to chamber the next. His right hand wrapped around the front of the stock, carved into basketweave and shaped like a pistol grip. He raised it, pressing the aluminum butt plate into his right shoulder and looked down the barrel aligning the sight with the eye of a hunter on a wall poster.

The pump action was for speed, the ability to rapidly re-chamber up to four cartridges while the trigger hand remained in place. An experienced shooter could get off five shots in as many seconds. Ray was concerned about quickly getting off a second shot, maybe a third if he needed it. He pumped the forearm through three cycles, the mechanism smooth in his hand, the metallic chuck-chuck sounding like no thing other than a cycling rifle.

"Well, what do you think, sir?" Gunner asked.

If Ray heard the question, there was no sign of it. He'd imagined his mission, what he'd come to see as his destiny, visualized it, elevated it to a certainty subject only to his will. Now, its instrument in his hands, he felt the murderous power of his intention and was surprised by his body. Not by the quickening in his chest or the flutter in his gut, but by the fullness in his groin. His penis swelled and he turned away from Gunner, swallowing a laugh. This fugitive, this armed robber, was no stranger to weapons or perverse arousal. But it wasn't the gun that was giving him the hard on, it was the thing he was intending.

Confident of the sale, Gunner let him be. Ray went through the motions of consideration—raising and lowering it from his shoulder, sighting down the barrel, chuck-chucking it a few more times. Finally he set it on the counter. "What'd you say the range of this gun is?"

"Well, the accurate range is about two hundred yards for an experienced shooter," Gunner said. "If you know what you're doing and you've got the right scope, you can keep a group within an inch or two at that distance. You gonna want me to mount the same scope as the one you brought back, the two-seven?"

He'd talked Ray through it the day before. The Redfield scope at its maximum 7x had a field of view of about six yards from a hundred yards distance. That meant that if he were standing on the goal line of a football field, the scope would be filled entirely with an area between the opposite five yard line and goal line, and a buck deer would occupy about a third of it. And it had a special coating on the glass that made it easier to see in low light. "If you can shoot straight at all," Gunner said, "the buck's kill zone, you know just behind the shoulder, should be easy."

He told him to go ahead and mount the scope on the thirty-aught-six. Gunner said it would take about an hour or so and Ray told him he'd be back in two. It was a warm early spring day and he rolled the windows down on the Mustang and headed out for a spin around Birmingham. He stopped at a burger joint and picked up two with "everything on 'em" and a Pepsi. Johnny Cash was on the cassette player and Ray one-handed the hardtop while he ate his lunch with the other. Johnny was singing "Mean as Hell" and Ray was thinking about only one thing and giving not a moment's thought to buck deer and shoulder shots.

It was Christmastime in the San Fernando Valley and the loner who despised crowds was in one. Seven months of restless flight and armed robbery had taken Ray from a roadside ditch in Jefferson City to St. Louis and Chicago, to Canada, down to Mexico and up to Los Angeles.

Amid a thousand or so pumped-up partisans on the infield of a Burbank stock car track, he awaited the arrival of George Wallace. He'd volunteered at his campaign headquarters in North Hollywood and was there to see the former governor and help collect signatures to get him on the California presidential primary ballot. A country band was warming up the crowd as he elbowed his way toward the edge of the makeshift stage. A bearded man in a biker jacket objected, "Hey asshole."

He pressed ahead, his hand on the grip of the Liberty Chief .38 revolver in his windbreaker pocket. It was a Japanese knock-off of the Colt Detective Special, the snub-nosed .38 caliber favorite of cops and crooks, small and easy to conceal, and powerful. His equalizer, he called it. Prison-hard and carrying, the only thing he feared was the police. Civilians were marks and pushovers.

He made it to the foot of the risers as Chill Wills, the Texas musician and movie actor, took the stage to introduce Wallace. Speeding on Dexedrine, Ray blinked and fidgeted and chewed his lip as Wills told his cornball jokes and hammed it up letting the crowd know that he was the voice of Francis the Talking Mule. There was scattered laughter, but Ray, humorless anyway, was mute and impatient. Finally the band struck up "Dixie" and Wills introduced the man that Ray had come to admire.

Wallace strutted out and Ray had the same thought about him that he had the first time he saw him up close. He reminded him of Jimmy Cagney—short, a half a foot shorter than Wills, with a big square head and a mug that said "Just try it, Buster." He'd been a professional boxer before law and politics and was fluent in the spoken and unspoken language of aggression and confrontation. Throughout his speech, his left fist was clenched, punctuating with hooks and jabs.

"And it is a sad day in our country," Wallace bellowed in a voice reserved for southern preachers and politicians, "that you cannot walk even in your neighborhoods at night or even in the daytime." He spoke through a fixed scowl, his eyes nearly black beneath thick arcuate brows. "Both national parties, in the last number of years, have kowtowed to every group of anarchists that have roamed the streets of San Francisco and Los Angeles and throughout the country."

Ray had begun paying attention to Wallace years before his national candidacy, before his "Segregation Forever!" was ciphered to "respect for states' rights," before his *nigra* became nee-groh. He particularly liked the story that young Wallace, after losing the first election of his career to a *more* segregationist opponent, swore that he'd never be "outniggered" again. He admired him, all right. And one day, Ray promised himself, that admiration would be returned.

The candidate turned up the volume. "And now they have created themselves a Frankenstein monster and the chickens are comin' home to roost all over this country. Yes, they've looked down their nose at you and me a long time. They've called us rednecks, the Republicans and the Democrats. Well, we're gonna show there sure are a lot of rednecks in this country."

The crowd erupted as Wallace knew they would. It was the line that ignited every crowd at every stump speech.

But Ray sat silent, a captive of his own joylessness. He did not share excitement, much less jubilation, about anything. What he shared with these people and with this fiery former governor was an enemy. He couldn't know and didn't care if Wallace was the real thing or just a politically expedient racist. What he was sure about was his own hatred. James Earl Ray was a racist to the bone.

"These'll mushroom to twice their size on penetration," Gunner said, cradling two cartridges in his palm.

They were almost done. The Redfield scope was affixed to the thirty-aught-six and all that was left was the choice of ammunition and settling up. Gunner told Ray that at a hundred yards these cartridges would generate about twelve hundred foot-pounds of energy on impact. Ray didn't know what that meant and had no interest in finding out.

"These are Peters?" Ray asked. "My brother told me to get Peters."

"Yes sir. These are Remington-Peters cartridges. Softpoints, high velocity. This is the right cartridge for this rifle."

He paid him in cash and put the rifle and a box of twenty cartridges in the trunk of the Mustang. Inside, he locked the door and sat stock still with his eyes closed. A passerby on foot thought it odd, a man sitting in a parked car like that in the middle of the day. He'd begun doing this in L.A., for minutes at a time motionless, envisioning scenes from his future. He'd read a book by a man named Maltz who preached that success required detachment from the past and single-minded action forward, a passionate attachment to what lay ahead. He believed this and returned again and again to the coming attractions of his imagination.

Pristine in a white tuxedo, he sits at a dinner table in the private residence. President Wallace, who has pardoned him, sits directly across. "The country is grateful to you," the president says, "for your courage and your service. You have lanced a boil, James, and excised from our midst the most dangerous man in America. You have my unending admiration and gratitude."

And now he's in the back seat of a grand convertible, horse guards to each side, gliding slowly down a broad boulevard lined with green and white flags and thousands of well-wishers smiling and cheering as he passes. Seated beside him is an elegant and angular gray-haired man, the Prime Minister. "As you can see, Mister Ray, you are a hero in Rhodesia. I trust that you will be happy with your choice to be one of us."

Ray opened the glove compartment, pushed aside the Liberty Chief .38 and pulled out his Georgia roadmap. On one side was the entire state. He traced US-78 coming due east out of Alabama and headed straight for Atlanta, about a three and a half hour drive from Birmingham. Then he flipped it over for the detailed Atlanta street map. On it are were three locations circled in red. They were roughly the points of a triangle, with each leg about three miles in length. The circle to the north was the ragged 14th Street rooming house which he'd occupied five days earlier and to which he was returning. The circle to the lower right was the intersection of Auburn Avenue and Jackson Street, the location of Ebenezer Baptist Church. The third circle, to the lower left, was the Sunset Avenue residence of the man he liked to call Martin Luther Coon. He intended to kill him in his home town.

March 31, Chicago

The barracks television set was on from early morning until the last medical student went to bed at night. Nick, Jeff and Larry were playing five card draw as the president started his televised Oval Office address. Amid the strewn remains of El Tacqueria take out, Nick half-listened, expecting nothing more than hollow condolences and stay-the-course bromides. Larry wasn't listening at all as he topped everyone's obstetrical adventure of the day with a play-by-play of the ritual sacrifice of a live chicken simultaneous with his delivery of a healthy baby girl. The executioner, the infant's Cuban grandmother, told him that the blood spurting from the creature's freshly cut throat would transmit the energy of life to the newborn baby. "She seemed quite sure about this," Larry said, tossing three cards in the pile in exchange for three more.

"Tonight I want to speak to you of peace in Vietnam and Southeast Asia."

"You're shitting us, right?" Jeff said, arranging and rearranging his cards to the annoyance particularly of Larry, who took his poker at least as seriously as his obstetrics.

"You've got five cards," Larry said, "five total cards. How many freakin' ways are there to arrange them? And no I'm not shitting you. She cut the chicken's throat with a carving knife, practically took it's hideous little head off."

"Now, as in the past, the United States is ready to send its representatives to any forum, at any time, to discuss the means of bringing this ugly war to an end."

Nick, who was dealing, responded to Jeff's long overdue request for two cards and dealt himself four, hoping to enhance a lonely black jack. Not a lover of the game, he played to fill the hours between cases and to be a good barracks mate. With the stakes low enough to make bluffing irrelevant, these poker games came down to little more than luck. About as interesting, he thought, as drawing straws. His game throughout medical school had been bridge, and before that gin rummy, his dad's game. As a little kid he'd sat on his father's lap when the regular penny-a-point foursome was in the dining room of their Rogers Park apartment. He learned about ginning and knocking and laying in wait with low points early in the hand. The price for this was his absolute silence during play, and a promise to keep the men's glasses filled with Canada Dry ginger ale, which he thought was somehow the official beverage of gin rummy. Meanwhile in the kitchen his mother and her friends played canasta or mah jongg, games he was as likely to engage in as jump rope or hopscotch.

"We have no intention of widening this war. Our objective in South Vietnam has never been the annihilation of the enemy."

After the draw, Nick's hand was just another iteration of jack high, Larry was looking smug, and Jeff hadn't let go of the chicken. "I'm trying to picture this," Jeff said. "Where exactly did she do this?" It seemed to Nick that Jeff was navigating somewhere between curious and skeptical.

"Over the kitchen sink," Larry said. "She had its body tucked under her armpit while holding it by the neck. After she slit its throat she just let go—the knife, the bird, the gushing blood dropping into the basin. She did it like she'd done it a thousand times. Christ, maybe she has."

Jeff was convinced. "Unbelievable," he said, with an intonation that meant just the opposite.

"One day, my fellow citizens, there will be peace in Southeast Asia."

The high point of Nick's day had been his encounter with Blossom Amos. It wasn't the stuff of poker table banter, and certainly couldn't compete with live animal sacrifice for the attention of his peers, but in it he unexpectedly made his way to the next level of his professional journey. He won the confidence of a patient who had walled herself off from every nurse, medical student, resident and attending physician who tried to get through to her. He had never in his brief medical career been the one, the one and only professional that a patient insisted upon. His identity, his doctorness, was ratified not by degree or title or the length of his white coat, but by how he was held by a patient. He was as proud as he was fearful, and too awash in the experience to discern the passage as he traversed it.

He threw in his woeful hand and watched Larry corral the pot.

"I believe that a peaceful Asia is far nearer to reality because of what America has done in Vietnam."

"You know, this is pretty crazy," Jeff said. "Animal sacrifices while we, the flagrantly unprepared, are on our own delivering babies. Am I the only one who thinks this whole thing is a little bit nuts?"

"I don't know," Larry said, his impatience transparent. "Can we just play cards?"

"No Jeff, you are not the only one," Nick said. "I know they've been doing this for seventy-five years, but that doesn't mean it's a good idea. I don't care about the chickens or any of the other crazy shit. I do care about the flagrantly unprepared part. I mean what the hell are we doing here? Am I really ready to deliver babies on my own? Are any of us?"

"Believing this as I do, I have concluded that I should not permit the Presidency to become involved in the partisan divisions that are developing in this political year."

Amid the cards and the conversation, the shift in Johnson's rhetoric registered with Nick. "Wait wait. I want to hear this," he said, turning toward the TV set.

"With America's sons in the fields far away, with America's

future under challenge right here at home, with our hopes and the world's hopes for peace in the balance every day, I do not believe that I should devote an hour or a day of my time to any personal partisan causes or to any duties other than the awesome duties of this office—the Presidency of your country.

Accordingly, I shall not seek, and I will not accept, the nomination of my party for another term as your President."

It was well after midnight and Nick was sleepless, thinking about the sadness of the president and about his own vulnerability to Vietnam. Broken by the war, LBJ had spoken to the country like a man talking to his grandchildren, slow and soft and kind. It seemed that at any moment his eyes would well with tears. Oddly, he had never appeared as appealing, as attractively groomed, as handsome as in his moment of ultimate submission.

Nick had seen him up close in the autumn of 1964 rolling down West Madison Street in a big and thoroughly buttoned-up Cadillac limo. The crowd, if you could call it that, was about three deep to see the man who had succeeded their murdered president. A banner on the Caddy read "All The Way With LBJ." In his campaign speeches he said that he was going to keep America out of Southeast Asia, that the South Vietnamese would defend their country themselves. Less than four years later, his prophecy was in ashes.

The telephone startled Nick back to his middle-of-the-night obligation. He got to it before the second ring, saving perhaps a drop of sleep for his medical student brethren. He was relieved at the details—an uncomplicated pregnancy at full term, a healthy twenty-four year-old woman with a two year-old daughter who'd been delivered easily, a tenement apartment across the street from the Maternity Center. He would do this with only a nursing student. If need be, help was a minute away. Still there was the insistent nag, the meddling of self-doubt. Nick, with his paper-thin experience, would for the first time be the senior person at a delivery. His cynicism infected his thoughts, more so in the immediacy of this case, but at some level in every waking moment.

When he arrived at the Center his insecurity was sidetracked by the knockout of a nursing student assigned to join him. A light-eyed blonde like most of her classmates from St. Olaf's College in Minnesota, this one—her name was Katherine Magnuson—was strikingly pretty, prom queen pretty. "Call me Kathy," she said as they were about to head out. "That's Kathy with a K." Her flirtation was perky, without a whiff of the prospect of disappointment.

This one was out to bag herself a young doctor, Nick thought, and he or any one of them could do a lot worse. He knew, though, that she was strictly off-limits and he had no interest in getting on the wrong side of Ernie, who was, among many other things, the guardian angel of the nursing students.

The downside of lovely Kathy's company was Nick's heightened anxiety over the delivery. He was nervous enough without having to worry about looking cool and competent for this beauty. But that concern evaporated the moment the door opened to their patient's apartment. A young man greeted them with only his eyes. He did not smile or speak, though there was nothing in his demeanor that was overtly threatening. He was very dark, almost black, afroed and about three inches taller than Nick. It must have been cold inside because he was wearing a knee-length leather coat, wide-lapelled with a large and unmistakable patch over the left breast pocket. He was Abrafo.

They followed him to a bedroom. "This is my sister," the young man said. "You take care of her." It wasn't a request.

"What's your name?" Nick asked him in the cheeriest voice he could muster.

The gang member controlled the moment with his silence. He looked to the side and down, then directly at Nick, stepping forward into a territory that should have been a no man's land. "What's yours?"

Nick told him and the gang member broke into a surprising smile, a broad incandescent genetically lucky display. His eyes, though, were not so versatile, his hardness not so readily camouflaged. "Weissman," he said, "Well, I guess that would make me Schwartzman."

Witless in his fear and awkwardness, Nick said nothing. The gang member let the tension slip. "You can call me Sonny."

Nick was surprised by his own sense of calm, or at least the absence of panic. They were not in the street, and Sonny had no "face" to preserve, no fellow Abrafo to impress. He was a gang member all right, but Nick chose to experience him as the patient's brother, the soon-to-be newborn's uncle, a young man committed to actual family, not just 'hood family.

Sonny's sister was Freddie, Winifred on her Maternity Center records. Nick and Kathy found her sitting up in bed, composed, at ease between contractions. The bedroom was pristine.

He introduced himself and asked Freddie about her family, expecting a grandmother, an aunt, a domestic resource responsible for the spotless surroundings. "It's just me and Sonny," Freddie said, "and James, my two year-old. He's with a neighbor."

Nick quickly went to his rote history-taking—the usual exploration of the what and when of the pregnancy and the progression of labor. Alongside that, though, there was a whisper of dissonance, something unexpected, out of order. He wouldn't ask, but he was left to assume that Sonny, a member of a badass gang and presumably a badass himself, was a first-rate housekeeper and likely a responsible partner in the care of his nephew.

From his physical exam, he estimated that Freddie's cervix was eighty percent dilated. Her contractions were about two minutes apart and he thought that she would deliver within an hour or two. Kathy started to ready the kitchen and Nick quietly talked Freddie from one contraction to the next. Sonny kept his distance in the living room.

Nick intended to re-examine Freddie after four more contractions, but the last of them was overdue. He waited ten nervous minutes and checked her cervix. She was still dilated eight centimeters. Her labor had stalled. He went into the living room and told Sonny that he needed to use the telephone. "What is it," Sonny said, "what's goin' on?"

"Her contractions stopped," Nick said. "I need to call

the Center."

Sonny pointed to a wall phone in the kitchen. As Nick dialed, Sonny edged within inches of him. Nick could smell the younger man's sweat.

The on-call attending physician at the Center was the boss, Teresa Butler. Nick was at once relieved and intimidated. She would know what to do. She asked him if he had Pitocin in his kit. "I do," he said, "but I've never used it on my own."

"You say you do have it?" she asked.

"Yes, I have it," he said, "but I'm a little, you know—"

"Don't do anything," she said. "I'll be there in five minutes."

Nick explained the situation to Freddie, who appeared to be calm and asked no questions. He looked for Sonny and found him in a second bedroom standing next to a tall chest of drawers. "Let me explain what's going on," Nick said. "It appears that—"

That's as far as he got, stopped in mid-sentence by a gun. Sonny's right arm was draped over the top of the chest, his hand resting a few inches from the handle of a dull silver revolver. "Go on," Sonny said, still quiet, overtly even-tempered.

Nick felt nauseous and he descended to a sitting position on the bed. Endangered animals do this, submit in reflex helplessness in hopes of being spared. He had no such thoughts, but his body did it. "Freddie's labor has stalled," he said. "Doctor Butler, the director of the Maternity Center, will be here in a few minutes."

"To do what?" Sonny asked.

"To be honest, I'm not sure. She might try to stimulate the labor here. She might put her in the hospital."

Sonny returned to silence. After an awkward delay, Nick stood slowly. "I'd better check on your sister," he said, and walked out of the room. He felt that he might lose his balance, as if his two feet on the floor were insufficient to contend with gravity. As he navigated from bedroom to bedroom, he placed the palm of his right hand flush to the wall. He made it to Freddie's side without a mishap.

"You feeling anything?" Nick asked her.

"Little pains," she said, "but nothin' that's gonna move this baby."

"Well, Doctor Butler's coming over," he said. "She's my boss, the lady who runs the Maternity Center. She'll be here any time now, and she'll find a way to get your labor going again." He sat at the foot of the bed and waited. He could feel Sonny behind him.

Teresa Butler, with Mary in tow, strode in like she owned the place. She walked past Sonny as if he were invisible. After the briefest of glances at Nick, she asked when he did his last exam.

"It's been about twenty minutes now," he said. "Still eight centimeters."

She snapped on a pair of gloves and did a quick assessment. "More like six to seven," she said. "Let's give her some Pit."

Pit was the Pitocin she'd asked about, an intravenous drug that Nick had seen used dozens of times in his hospital obstetrics rotations. It strengthened uterine contractions and was the drug of choice for stimulating labor.

Butler was explaining the Pitocin treatment to Freddie, and Mary was hanging a bottle of saline, leaving Nick to start the IV. Despite his anxiety, he did it on the first try on the back of her right hand.

Butler's rescue mission was, for her, routine, one of a thousand such remedial interventions—simple, effortless, forgettable. For Nick, her arrival was a blessing and a curse, a clinical necessity and evidence of his inadequacy, a relief and a failure. Sonny's pistol gambit aside, this was not an extraordinary case. The slowing of labor and the use of Pitocin were common and routine. He could have done it on his own or with telephone consultation. But he hesitated and Butler gave him no slack at all. He'd missed his independent moment.

Freddie's labor pains resumed within a few minutes of the Pitocin administration, and Butler abruptly pushed Nick back to center stage for the delivery. "She's still your patient, doctor," she said, retreating to the back of the makeshift labor room. Now he'd have to do this under Butler's direct surveillance, as if he needed another quantum of anxiety.

Mary pitched in with Kathy-with-a-K to finish getting the kitchen ready. The newspaper rolls were prepped and the instruments were laid out from the travel kit. A wall hook and a coat hanger were fashioned to receive the IV bottle. Nick was timing the contractions and monitoring fetal heart tones and Butler was reading a paperback. With Butler's arrival Sonny had receded into the background, sitting in the living room and occasionally peeking in on his sister. He'd been soft spoken, even in his threat. An odd one, brandishing the symbols of aggression without aggression itself or even the sense of its imminence. The Abrafo coat, the gun, then the passivity.

Despite the circumstances, Nick found his footing. When Freddie's contractions were a minute apart, he walked her into the kitchen himself, recruiting Sonny, who'd been checking in on his sister, to bring along the IV bottle. Butler kept on reading in the bedroom, as if she were in her parlor in her pajamas.

The delivery could not have been easier, a sit-there-and-try-not-to-drop-the-baby event, without further delay or complication. It was a girl and she wailed immediately. In short order Nick dried her off with a towel, cut the cord, handed her off to Kathy-with-a-K, and delivered the placenta. His anxiety evaporated. His fears—of being on his own, of contending with Sonny, of failing with Butler—dissipated with the hearty howl of this newborn baby.

Nick placed the infant girl on her mother's chest. Freddie held her comfortably, rocking her and tracing the contours of her face with her fingers. Sonny was leaning in, his index finger locked in the hand of his brand new niece.

Nick took stock of the young man. He'd shed his Abrafo jacket and was dressed black-on-black, jeans and a tight tee shirt. He looked like he pumped iron, with biceps and delts that were defined and big and veiny. His hard body, though, was not a match for the softness now of his expression, his eyes. He was *en face* with his niece, his face lined up with hers. Nick watched and understood that this was how humans bonded with newborns, this was what falling in love looked like.

Sonny was a contradiction, a possibly homicidal gang member and a protective and loving brother and uncle, a cut stud and a doughy-eyed pushover. An odd inkling was pushing its way into Nick's awareness, a seed of doubt, a suspicion about the trustworthiness of his senses. He fought it off. He was not crazy and he did not believe in magic, black or otherwise. He did not hear voices or see things that were not there. Still, there was the uninvited whisper that his fearful imagination had tricked him.

He walked alone into the second bedroom, the one where Sonny had stood next to the tall dresser. There was no gun. Well, so what, Nick thought. Surely he wouldn't leave it sitting out there. He put it away, he must have put it away.

In the Loop

Nick was ready for steak. The taxi ride from the barracks to Pierre's, his father's restaurant, would traverse about three miles and a yawning divide—of wealth, race, and safety. He was ready for a break from the Maternity Center grind, for a few hours of normal, and for a decent meal. His call surprised his mother, who without hesitation shuffled her schedule for the uncommon opportunity to have dinner with her son.

Pierre's was in the Loop, Chicago's downtown district, named for its complete encirclement by the el, the city's commuter rail system. As the cab crawled through late afternoon rush hour traffic, Nick sat in the back, eyes closed, recapturing an evening that he had not thought about in years.

In a low-lit alcove opposite the bar, Nicky looks up from

119

his menu at the two suit-and-ties, three stools apart sipping and smoking. Alfrieda, who had held him as an infant, stands pen-poised in her horn-rimmed glasses, shiny black polyester zip-up, and white apron. She watches him sitting there by himself, aswallow in the maroon leather of the brass-tacked booth and the layers of linen. "I think I'll have the Caesar salad," Nicky finally says, "and a filet mignon medium rare with onion rings and some creamed spinach." He's twelve.

Despite the restaurant's name, there is nothing French about it, and as far as anyone knows, no one named Pierre had anything to do with it. Grandpa Abe had staked his two young and hustling salesman sons-in-law, Nick's father and uncle, to something of their own. Nicky began working there when he was eleven, summers and holiday breaks and sometimes after school, mostly greeting and seating, sometimes cashiering. A little man all dressed up, he is pretty good at it, charming the amused and forgiving customers. Benign and barely conscious, it is nonetheless his preadolescent initiation to audacity as a career strategy. A dozen years later, he and his fellow medical students will be at it in spades—see one, do one, teach one—imposters in white, every one of them.

He finishes his meal and relieves his father at the register. He is allowed to handle the money only for the dinner shift. At ground zero of Chicago's downtown financial district, Pierre's seats nearly three hundred eaters at a time, and fortunately for the family it roars at breakfast and lunch. Dinner is different—fewer and less frenetic patrons, a slower turnover—so Nicky gets his chance in the more responsible role. Still, his father hovers. Be careful. Take your time. Don't be such a big shot. Always the double message.

It's easy. Nearly everyone pays in cash, and for the occasional personal check or Diner's Club card he gets a scribbled "OK" from Dad. The pale green checks are generated by the waitresses and as each is paid, he impales it on a metal spike atop its predecessors. The next business day, the accounting department (his father and his hand-cranked adding machine) reconciles, artfully Nick later learns, the pierced pile of paper with the pile of cash. Accounts receivable circa 1956.

Pierre's is also his initiation to celebrity. For the first time and up close, he gets to see the famous, at least the Chicago famous. Irv Kupcinet of the Sun-Times, eventually the Methusalah of local gossip columnists, is a regular. So is George "Papa Bear" Halas. The Bears' administrative offices are in the same building as the restaurant, upstairs on the eighth floor, and Halas and his staff come down for a meal two or three times a week. He once saw Sid Luckman, the legendary quarterback—and Jewish, his father never fails to remind him—sitting with Halas and the coaches. And there are plenty of politicians, the most venerable of whom is Jacob "Jack" Arvey, a State Senator who, even in the epoch of Mayor Richard J. Daley, is the most influential man in the *realpolitik* of the Illinois Democratic Party.

In the 1950's the Toddlin' Town is as crooked as its meandering river. The police, the unions, the Mob and the politicians are practically seamless and utterly shameless. It seems as though everyone is on the take. If you're stopped for speeding, the officer looks at your license, tells you how fast you were going, and bored and impatient—hey, this is a volume business—asks, "So what do you wanna do?"

Cops and crooks join forces in complex, ongoing criminal operations, from car-towing, chop-shop disassembly lines to home burglary, fence distribution networks. Millions a year, stolen, laundered and taxed (no, not by the IRS). The insurance companies can afford it, right? What's the big deal? In the most infamous police debacle of the era, the "Summerdale Scandal," a second story man named Richie Morrison—the "Babbling Burglar," to the Chicago press corps—blew the whistle on an entire felonious precinct, ending the careers of several senior officers including the Chief of Police, and nearly took down Hizzonor Da Mayor himself. Corruption and extortion are rampant, woven into the everyday business of the city. The passports to legitimate livelihood—the permits, licenses, service contracts, labor agreements—are as a matter of routine held hostage to bribe and threat. In mid-century Chicago, intimidation and the greased palm rule. Unexceptional, ordinary, nearly everything is oiled, and soiled.

The Pierre's Liquor License Shakedown of 1954 is already a family legend. Nicky's father tells it about like this, and often:

> *"It's lunchtime, the place is absolutely packed. Every table, every counter seat, a dozen or so waiting. It's maybe 12:30. I'm hosting, seating, kibitzing, nothing unusual. This guy comes in, at first looks like an ordinary customer, brown suit, brown hat, shirt and tie. He walks directly to a table in the back of the front dining*

room and I don't know why, but I get a bad feeling. (Nicky thought his old man, not noted for his intuition, was embellishing here.) He's immediately talking to a girl at the table, she shows him something from her purse, and he turns around and heads straight for me. Mr. Weissman, he says. Jesus, he knows my name. I'm thinking, what the hell? Mr. Weissman, I don't want to embarrass you. Is there some place we can talk? As he says this, with a flip of the hand he shows me a badge and puts it back in his pocket. I ask him what this is about and he insists that we go somewhere to talk. So I take him upstairs to my office and he sits down and says, Mr. Weissman, you're serving alcohol to a minor. You served a martini to that nineteen year-old girl. I tell him we card everybody. He says he's sorry, but she's nineteen and she's drinking a martini in my restaurant. Then he gives me this long look and tells me that he's sure we can work something out, that it would be a shame if Pierre's lost its liquor license over a simple mistake. That's what he called it, a simple mistake. I'd call it a put-up job, a fucking shakedown. I don't say a word. He stares at me for a few seconds more and then he takes a folded piece of paper from his shirt pocket and hands it to me. I look at it. It says, five thousand dollars cash. Five thousand dollars! I'll wait, he says. You'll wait for what, I ask. For the cash, he says. You mean, right now? That's right, he says. Jesus Christ, you're not serious. He just stares at me. I feel like I'm going to throw up. (Nicky said that there was some variation to this part of the story; sometimes his father described going to the bathroom and throwing up.) I tell him that he has to wait in the outer office while I make a phone call. He doesn't like it but he goes. The call is to Senator Arvey. Thank god I reach him and explain what's going on. If he can't help me, nobody can. He says he'll make a few calls and get right back to me. Ten minutes later the phone rings and it's the Senator. Jack, he says, pay 'em."

The dinner crowd has thinned out, the hum and clatter of seven o'clock giving way to the single voices and collisions of closing time—one cup aclink on one saucer, a discernible fork arriving with an echo on a dessert plate. Chin on his fists, Nicky waits for the lingering few to finish, to drink their coffee and smoke their last smoke and give him their money and let Dad take him home. The air is thick with cigarette and cigar and pipe and charred meat and tomorrow morning's pastry dough. The little man is just about finished. If only he could rest his head on the cashier's counter, he'd be asleep in seconds.

They burst in from his right, four of them through the front revolving door, two in suits and two in uniform. In the same moment, irregular pulses of dark red light fill the front of the restaurant. Through the tinted glass facade, he can make out at least two cherry-tops at the curb, Chicago's Finest. Now he's wide awake. The four policeman, just short of running, hie it through the main dining room and the back bar, and disappear through the metal swinging doors into the kitchen. His father, who had moments earlier been schmoozing a regular, is standing next to him. "What the hell's going on?" Nicky shrugs his shoulders. Side by side, silent, they stand there.

The suits, detectives he figures, emerge first, then the two uniformed officers with their captive. They have him at the crook of each elbow. In busboy attire—black shoes, black slacks, starched white collarless jacket—he walks head down, his pomade wavy hair under a standard fishnet cover-up. He's cuffed behind his back. As the police guide their prisoner past the cashier's counter, Nicky's father says it exactly as he has been saying it for as long as Nicky can remember. "Goddamn *schvartzes.*"

Schvartze, Nicky understands, is Yiddish for nigger.

He greeted his mother with a hug and a kiss on the cheek. Tally Weissman at fifty-five was still a beauty, her white hair setting off her dark eyes and olive skin. Nick had never waded into the contradiction that the exotic Sephardic palette that he found so beautiful in his mother was the very thing he'd for so long abhorred in himself.

"Nicky, you look like you could use some sleep."

"That's been true since pre-med, mom. Sit down, I'll buy you a drink."

They would, of course, not be buying anything. Between Pierre's and Barron's, his grandparents' West Side deli, the Weissmans had been dining out and carrying out *gratis* for decades. The family freezer fairly burst with steaks and chops and slabs of kosher corned beef and pastrami. From the time he could chew, Nick had been accustomed to choice and prime, to lobster tail and rack of lamb, to a rich man's bounty on a middle class kitchen table.

"I'm just saying you look tired," she said. "And pale."

"Pale? I never look pale. I'm fine, mom. Really."

Had he a skull-crushing migraine, an abdomen on fire with dyspepsia, an ingrown toenail, anything, it would not be revealed. His mother's anxiety was too high a price for whatever tenderness might come his way. He was, in fact, sleep deprived, moving through his Maternity Center days and nights in a gauzy shroud of fatigue, his attention, his memory, his reaction times eroded enough to deprive him of the crispness of real time. Not just tired in the ordinary sense, sleepy, but a moment or two behind the moments.

There was catch-up from mom, the Jewish news. Uncle Harry and Aunt Ethel were in Miami Beach. Cousin Ronnie made the tennis team in Madison. Saul Bernstein got a new Coupe de Ville. Nick knew that her recitation was preamble. It barely made it into one ear, much less out the other. Nick's old man was blunt. No one ever accused Jack Weissman of finesse. But his mother had a sense of pace, a rhythm to her conversational journey. After some more on the *mishpachah* and a detour through her volunteer work at the Art Institute, she made her way to the territory of her interest.

"So tell me a little about what you're doing," she said, as though it were just one more item in a casual inventory.

Starting around seventh grade, when Nick began a clandestine life in earnest, smoking cigarettes, paying sexual attention to girls, masturbating, he also began what would become over the years a refined and habitual parsing of information. This was not lying, exactly, but selective conceal-ment, at times to authentically protect his parents from un-necessary worry, at least as often to protect himself—from intrusiveness, from judgment, from accountability. He was not a blurter.

"The Maternity Center is really a neighborhood clinic," he said. "We see prenatal visits and there are half days where we do check-ups on the newborns. Most of it is uncomplicated. It's kind of repetitive."

By now there was a wedge of iceberg lettuce smothered in thousand island dressing in front of him, its forkfuls punctuating his casual misdirection. He didn't manufacture his benign details. There were routine clinics, uneventful pregnancies, healthy babies, and rote instructions. There were evenings of nothing but TV, poker, monopoly, and rock 'n roll.

His mother continued her excavation. "Uh huh, so what happens when these girls go into labor?"

"Well, it depends," he said. "Every case is a little different. The complicated cases go to the hospital, almost always Cook County. We do the low-risk cases."

"And by do, you mean you go out and do the deliveries."

'Yeah, we do the deliveries."

"In the homes, the apartments, the tenements."

"Right."

Not every home delivery was harrowing, not every neighborhood horrifying, but he knew where this was headed. Her fears were his fears, but he would manage the moment, or try. In most respects his mother was nothing like his father. She was civil, respectful, a word like schvartze would never cross her lips. She was a Kennedy Democrat, a civil rights advocate. She'd treated Effie, his childhood caretaker, like a member of the family. Still, there was the fear, some of it realistic, and the soft bigotry that he knew he shared.

"So who goes with you on these deliveries?" she asked.

"Well, it varies," he said, heading for the safety of medical detail. "If it's a simple uncomplicated case, a nurse or sometimes a nursing student. If there's some reason for concern, a complication—but not serious enough to send them directly to the hospital—then a resident or the medical director will come. I just had a case where the labor slowed down near the end and Doctor Butler, the medical director, came out and supervised. I started an IV drip of this drug called Pitocin that causes the uterus to contract. And it worked."

His mother, by outward appearance, had been listening, interested. "And who else?"

"Who else what?" he said, with a quiet pretense of confusion.

"Who else goes with you on the deliveries?"

"Like I said, it depends on the complexity of the case."

He prepared a dinner roll, his thumbs side by side piercing the crust, eyes fixed on the task like he was repairing a watch. After painting a dollop of butter on each torn half, he set the knife down, took a bite, and looked up. His mother was waiting.

"You're asking about protection," he said, "about whether someone is with us who can protect us when we go out on these cases. Is that what you're asking?" .

Only the inner family circle—Nick, his sister, his father—would have likely deciphered the halting toothless smile, the fraction of a squint, the topography of Tally Weissman's veiled irritation.

"I'm out of line?" she said, as though it were a question. "It's somehow wrong for me to be worried about your safety?" Acquiring momentum, she shed the veil. "Are you going to make me feel bad for asking?"

This was a button pushed, the trillionth "be careful," the burden of disingenuous explanation, the ready-to-feel-guilty-at-the-drop-of-a-hat anyway, all magnified by his knowing that she was fucking right to be scared for him, and that a breath of confirmation would shatter whatever reassurance he was about to serve up.

He was buttering again. Another smear, another bite. "No, I'm not trying to make you feel bad," he said, his thoughts navigating first to the unmentionables—Bobby Plunkett's mugging, the intimidation by the Abrafo, Sonny's gun. Out of the question. He understood that there was only one way to have a shot at dealing with her fear, or at least to get out of this conversation. He would lie.

"In the dangerous neighborhoods, the police escort us in," he said, knowing that on the Near West Side there were only two kinds of neighborhoods—dangerous and more dangerous. And despite the stated policy of the Maternity Center, escorts by law enforcement were hardly routine. There'd been only one that he knew of since his rotation began.

"Really, every time?" she asked.

That's the thing about lying, once you start.

"Yeah, if we ask, they come."

"And they stay there with you?"

"Well, they can't stay with us. The visits can take hours. But they'll escort us back when we're done." Nick thought that mixing in a molecule of truth would somehow make it credible.

"So you're telling me that there's nothing to worry about," she said, "that the most dangerous neighborhoods in Chicago pose no threat to you at all, that I'm worrying for nothing."

"I'm telling you I'm fine," he said. "We're all fine. In a week the rotation will be over and you can stop your worrying. Now can we talk about something else?"

"Look, Nicky, I think you're being pretty cavalier about this. You know, I—"

"Please, mom. Stop it. The Maternity Center has been doing this for seventy-five years and everyone has survived. I came here tonight for a break, to see you and have a nice dinner. So please just stop. Okay?"

The dinner went on, but not the electric thread of the conversation. He'd slammed the door hard enough to keep it closed for the time being, though his unacknowledged risk and her unassuaged fear hung between them like barbed wire. He would not scare her out of her wits and she would not call her only son, the almost doctor, a liar to his face.

Nick and his mother small-talked their way through a pair of sirloins, and for dessert neglected most of the strawberry cheesecake, which according to Jack Weissman was the best in Chicago.

Southwest Tennessee

Ray held the Remington steady, ready to absorb its recoil into the layers of his bulky sweater and leather jacket. As a teenager in the Army at the end of World War II, he'd fired the M1 in basic training and knew the sound and kick of a high caliber rifle. Two decades later in the southwest Tennessee countryside, he embraced his weapon offhand in the standing position, sighting a red paper target that he'd tacked to a tree trunk some fifty yards away. He was in the woods just south of Shiloh, amid scattered stands of oak and hickory and pine in the low rolling hills that slope into the Tennessee River. He was facing west, Mississippi not much more than a stone's throw to his left and Memphis dead ahead, three hours by car.

His last seventy-two hours had been restless and fruit-less. After returning to Atlanta from Birmingham with the rifle and cartridges, he spent his days driving hour upon hour past Ebenezer Baptist and the Sunset house hoping to get a glimpse of King. At night he found his way to the bars and strip clubs where he was in his element, drinking alone and sizing up the women. Ray had a penchant for the underbelly of any city he inhabited, for the seediest motels and rooming houses, the cheapest bars, the easiest sex.

He was vigilant about his prey, scanning the newspapers, radio and television. Then, in an article in the Atlanta Constitution, he learned that King was leaving Atlanta for Memphis to support that city's striking sanitation workers, almost all of whom were black. King had gone there and marched with them a few days earlier, but the effort erupted into a street riot at the hands of outside agitators. He pledged to return to march with them again, and he was keeping his promise. King would go back to Memphis, the newspaper reported, on April third. Ray left Atlanta for Tennessee in his white Mustang in the early morning hours of April second.

He slowly squeezed the trigger, but the target seemed undisturbed through the scope. The ground was winter hard under his feet as he walked toward the tree, the Remington slung over his forearm. Up close he confirmed that he had missed.

The first time he fired a rifle he was eight. It was his father's .22. They'd go to the edge of a lake, just north of their Missouri home town. His father, an ex-con himself, showed him how to hold the rifle, aim, and properly squeeze the trigger. They'd stroll the water's edge in search of frogs and water snakes. He was thrilled at his first kill, a bloated bullfrog from ten yards away. His father told him it was nothing, that anybody could have done it.

He paced off another fifty yards to a fallen tree trunk close to where he had taken the shot. Laying prone on the ground, he rested the Remington's barrel on the bark of the tree and sighted through the scope and squeezed. This time the red paper jumped. The target was penetrated almost dead center. Now he knew he could shoot this weapon accurately, and he knew that the rifle would have to be stabilized when the moment came to take the shot. He'd used two cartridges, three were left in the magazine.

He made one more stop on his way to Memphis, a short side trip to the Shiloh battlefield and cemetery. A cell mate at Jeff City, a good old boy from Pulaski, Tennessee, the birthplace of the Ku Klux Klan, talked about it all the time. "It's a fuckin' disgrace," he told Ray. "Those nigger lovin' union boys each got their own grave, even if they was unknowns. If you was Johnny Reb, you're in a mass grave with hundreds of other Johnny Rebs."

Ray liked history, his version of it anyway. Lincoln was the enemy, ugly, hairy, likely some kind of mongrel. The civil war was a war against the white man. It was mass murder, a brutal assault on the proper order of things. The defeat of the Confederacy meant that America would forever be poisoned by an inferior race. For him, going to Shiloh served up an extra helping of hate, further proof of the rightness of his mission. He spent two hours there and got what he wanted.

The Battle of Shiloh, fought in the early spring of 1862, was the bloodiest battle in American history up to that time—two days of fighting with roughly 25,000 casualties, 3,500 dead. It was the Confederate Army's effort to prevent the North from gaining a foothold in Mississippi.

Ignited by a disorganized but successful surprise attack by the the South on April 6, it ended with an overwhelming counter-offensive the next day by heavily reinforced Union soldiers.

Ray went first to the cemetery, a burial ground exclusively for the Union fallen. The setting was idyllic, manicured grass, tall shade trees over precisely spaced markers, like little stone soldiers in perfect formation spilling into the west bank of the Tennessee River. The gravestones were in straight rows and in arcs. The unknowns, which predominated, were marked with simple numbered cubes, the knowns with engraved taller archtop stones.

He paced the lanes between the markers, the elegance and serenity serving only to fuel his resentment. He thought the honoring of the Yankee victors was an atrocity, a celebration of the soiling of America. The country had lost its way a century earlier, and was getting worse. Something had to be done.

From the cemetery he drove two miles southwest to the site of the Methodist meeting house that gave its name to the battlefield. The log church, no longer standing, was called Shiloh, a Hebrew word meaning, of all things, a place of tranquility. Most of the Confederate soldiers who fought there died there. They were buried en masse in a hole in the ground a hundred yards to the east. Ray could see its demarcations from where he stood next to the Mustang.

He walked across an open field sloping downward and to the right, past a battery of four cannons, and stopped at a row of cannon balls lying on the ground. They formed the northern border of a rectangle made of single cannon balls, ten yards on the short side, forty yards on the long. A small sign on the long western side read "Confederate Burial Trench."

He thought these patriots were treated like garbage, swept into the dirt like trash at a town dump. His cell mate had captured it perfectly. This was a place of the devil, where evil lived amid elegant trees, sinuous hillsides, martial monuments, and a shimmering river. It was, Ray thought, a well-concealed monstrosity. He would leave it behind and complete his mission. Then he would leave his country behind.

Lamar Avenue is a main Memphis drag, cutting diagonally southeast from downtown. Ray drove it slow, looking for suitable lodging—cheap, low profile, blue collar. He'd come into the city on Tennessee Route 15 from Shiloh. It took him downtown, where he found a basement dive for dinner, ribs and fries and three cups of coffee. The bartender there directed him to the motels lining Lamar.

Cruising in the Mustang, he was body tired from his long day, but wired on caffeine and anticipation. The avenue was mostly commercial, strip malls and chain stores, fast food joints and gas stations. On the left side a marquee caught his eye.

OPEN NOON 'TIL 3 AM
– 3 COLOR FEATURES NOW -
$5 COUPLES $6

It was the Airway Theater, a pink and purple bricked

movie house which he could not pass up. He fancied himself a connoisseur of pornography, and had even entertained the idea of getting into the industry. He owned a Kodak Super 8 camera, a dual projector, and a splicing machine, and he had a collection of sex manuals and toys, and piles of porno magazines. He knew that the stuff in theaters was soft core, but it was better than nothing.

He sat in an empty row near the back of the main floor. He liked to be alone in these places, in the dark, undiscoverable. Porn houses were the best, and this one was nicer than most, large with a star-filled ceiling and dark red velvet seats, likely a first-run palace in its heyday. It was after eleven, and he could make out only two other men in the theater.

The action wasn't scintillating, but it was enough to get him going. College girls at a party dancing with their boyfriends, at first fully clothed, then in their bras and panties, then bare breasted. In the shadows there was simulated feeling up and going down, indistinct, genitalia cloaked. Ten minutes in, Ray was half hard and bored with the sexual fakery.

He found the men's room, locked himself in one of the stalls, and unrolled and tore off a large wad of toilet paper. He took some measure of pride in his hygiene and assumed that the men who came to this place were dirtier than him, maybe colored, maybe diseased. He wiped the toilet seat hard. Then he got another handful and wiped it again. He sat, his pants at his ankles, and closed his eyes..

These moments began any which way, with whatever got him started—porn, a hot memory, real or embellished, a sweeping archive of fantasies. But no matter where he began, when he tired of the slow climb, of the waiting, he turned time and again to the scene that he knew he could count on.

They are always against a wall, the white woman pinned, one leg fully extended over the man's shoulder. Ray sees him from behind, driving into her, the muscles of his back and his legs bulging under his brown-black skin.

There's a weapon in Ray's hand, the kind they used in Jeff City. Eight inches of rusty scrap metal, electrical tape for a handle and sharpened to a point. He steps behind the man and shanks him in the side, stabbing him six times in two seconds. The man gasps and falls and Ray pounces and slashes his throat. The naked woman is on her knees, screaming. He drops the blood-soaked weapon and wraps both hands around her neck. She is fouled and deserves to die.

He's got her on her back, her shoulders pinned beneath his knees. He feels her adam's apple crack as he drives his thumbs deep into the center of her neck. Her eyelids fall and the skin of her face goes a pale purple-gray.

This was always his moment. He was clutching himself, not stroking but squeezing with the force of the strangler. And like every other time, he was finished in seconds, ejaculating into the palms of his hands, his cum, he imagined, mixing with the blood of his victims.

He stepped onto the sidewalk in front of the theater, his day's exhaustion unleashed. He'd take the first motel, the first bed he could find.

"Hey mister," the woman said. "Mister!"

She was behind and to his left. He turned and took her in, everything except her eyes. She was tall and would have been even without her five inch heels. An ankle length fur coat was open enough to expose her cleavage and an amount of thigh that left no room for speculation. Her hair was an alien shade of yellow, short, and anchored by large brassy hoops that kissed her collar. Under scarlet gloss, her lips dominated a pretty milk chocolate face.

"How are ya tonight," she said.

Ray had nothing against hookers. His kind worked the downscale bars, where they cranked up the tabs for the watered down drinks, and took the big tippers into the back rooms for a tug or a blow job. And his kind were always white, the trashier the better.

"Ya wanna party? I got a place." She said it in a stage whisper, her coat falling further open as she stepped toward him, an arm's length away.

Spent or not, his prison wariness kicked in, the scanning vigilance that survival required. To his right, across the street in front of his Mustang, a man sat behind the wheel of a black Mercury sedan. He was looking straight at Ray and the woman. He was her driver or her pimp, he thought, or both. Or maybe this was something else.

"You'll like it, I promise," she said.

Ray felt for the wooden handle of the pistol in the deep right hand pocket of his leather jacket.

"Really," she said, "it'll be real good. I'll do whatever you want."

He imagined killing both of them, to rid the world of them. He'd play along, walk to the Mercury with her and get in. Once inside, the shots would be muffled. He'd do her pimp in the back of the head and savor the girl's horror before shoving the snub nose between her big lips and blowing her brains all over the upholstery. They deserved it, he was sure of that, just like the man in Puerto Vallarta deserved it.

It started in a working class Mexican bar a few months after his escape from Jeff City. Ray had been eying a man a few tables away, irritated, feeling that he contaminated the place. The man was one of the local Brazilian laborers, he thought, Spanish speakers with skin as black as pitch. Spic niggers, he called them. This one was loud, a little drunk, but not more than the rest of the crowd. Ray was on a bar stool matching vodka shots with an off-duty waitress when the man brushed against her as he walked past. When he doubled back a few minutes later, he did it again, this time flagrantly, sliding by sideways with his pelvis pushing hard against the woman's back side.

Ray was not a hot head—he burned slow and deliberate. When the man left the bar, he followed on foot at a distance, waiting for the opportunity to get him alone. He wanted to humiliate him, to make him fear for his life, to beg, to display his inferiority. As he trailed him down the street, his hand on the grip of the .38 revolver in his jacket pocket, he had not yet decided to execute him.

The man turned into a dark narrow unpaved alley way. Ray followed, edging carefully around the corner. The man was ten yards ahead of him. "Alto," Ray said. The man kept walking. "Alto," this time louder. The man stopped and turned. The pistol was out and pointed at the man's chest.

"Pesos," Ray said, gesturing "gimme" with the motion of his wrist. The man reached into his pants pocket, pulled out a thin wad of wrinkled bills and dropped them on the dirt. He glared at Ray and started to turn to walk away. "Alto." Ray said it quietly.

Had the man submitted to Ray's instruction, had he gotten to his knees and apologized for touching the woman, had he begged for his life, perhaps Ray would not have shot him, first in the chest, then in the throat.

He reminded himself why he was in Memphis, that he was there to do one thing only, that nothing else mattered. He spoke with his eyes averted enough to see the Mercury. "Go tell your friend to drive away."

"Hey, come on mister. I'll show you a real good time."

"Tell him to get out of here," Ray said, "right now."

"But don't you wanna have some fun?"

He took the pistol out and held it at his side in plain sight. The girl stepped back and he looked directly at her. "I'd rather fuck my dog," he said. "Now go tell your friend to drive away."

The click of the woman's heels echoed off the pavement as she crossed Lamar Avenue, late night empty now, lit only by the theater marquee. Ray watched her say something to the driver of the Mercury, then walk around the front of the car and get in. He waited until they pulled away and were out of sight before heading for the Mustang.

The One

In his first waking moments, Nick didn't know where he was. "C'mon," the voice said. It was a man's voice. "C'mon, ya gotta get up." There was shaking, a hand on his shoulder, his upper body in small oscillation. He opened his eyes enough to see Bobby Plunket leaning over him.

"What time is it?"

"A little before five," Bobby said.

Something was amiss. Even in his early morning haze, Nick knew that he wasn't supposed to be next up, not even close. When you're next up you sleep with the door open so that you can hear the telephone in the hallway. And it's a different kind of sleep, a sleep that expects to be interrupted.

"Why did you wake me? What's going on?"

"I really didn't want to," Bobby said, "but this family, this patient, says you're the only one she'll see. She's insisting. She says you promised you'd come when she called."

Nick was up on his elbows, still not piecing it together.

141

"What's her name?"

"Amos. Blossom Amos."

Blossom, his only Blossom. "I shouldn't make promises like that," Nick said, sitting up now, his feet on the floor. "She's got twins."

"How much time do you need?"

"If it's not urgent, tell them a half an hour."

"Really," Bobby said.

"All right, fifteen minutes."

"If she's actually in labor, we get her straight to County." Nick, with a leather satchel in each hand, was leading Mary through the front door as he spoke. "We call Wong, and we get her on her way." The obstetrics resident had been adamant about Blossom. This one delivers in the hospital, he'd said.

The building was a brown brick three-story six-flat, with a central front entrance and stairway. In the rear there was a network of wooden porches and steps descending to the alley below. Inner-city Chicago was the home to thousands of residential buildings exactly like it. This one was on Congress Street, facing the Eisenhower Expressway, within blocks of where Nick spent the first seven years of his life.

They reached the third floor landing, knocked, and waited. Nick was about to try again when he heard metal on metal, the undoing of three locks. Expecting Blossom's sister Caroline to open the door, it was instead a school age boy. "My mom's in the kitchen."

"You must be Charles," Nick said.

"How'd you know that?"

"Well, I know your mom and your Aunt Blossom too. I'm Nick and this is Mary."

"What are those?" the boy asked, pointing to one of the satchels.

"That's just stuff to help us take care of Blossom and her babies."

"What kinda stuff?"

"Doctor stuff, you know—"

"This boy'll talk you 'til midnight," Caroline Amos said, walking toward them. "Come on in. Charles, you go watch TV with your brother."

Nick led Mary in. Anxious as ever about his obstetrical shortcomings, he was confident at least of his acceptance and safety with this little family, and comforted by Mary's presence. Though unspoken, they both understood that she was his lifeline.

After hurried introduction of the two woman, Nick asked about Blossom. "She's havin' some contractions, I think," Caroline said, "some kinda pains anyway, but they haven't been real steady."

He quickly went through the standard questions about early labor. The frequency of contractions, the intervals between. Had her water broken? Was she bleeding? He was fluent, his insecurity residing not in the history-taking but in the laying on of obstetrical hands. His initial impression, before even seeing her, was that she was probably not in labor. No water, no blood, no regular pains.

"Hello Blossom, this is Mary," he said, standing at the foot of her bed.

Blossom, who'd been slouched, propped herself to an upright sitting position and smiled. She was wearing powder blue flannel pajamas adorned with circus animals. "Hi Doctor Weissman" she said, as though Mary were invisible. "Thanks for comin'. I thought maybe you weren't gonna keep your promise."

"Now why would you think that?" Nick said, starting to unpack one of the satchels.

"'Cause lotsa people don't keep their word. Jimmy promised he was gonna stick by me. It's his babies too, but I ain't seen him in months." As quickly as it had appeared, Blossom's smile was gone, replaced by the flatness, the deadness, that he had seen when he first met her in the clinic. "People don't do what they say they're gonna do. That's just how it is."

"Well, that's not how it is today," Nick said. "Mary and I are here to take care of you and your babies."

He repeated his due diligence with Blossom, confirming that her water had not broken and that there was no vaginal bleeding. She described her pains as cramps, pointing to the center of her belly. The last one had stopped about ten minutes earlier. She wasn't sure how long it lasted. "I don't know," she said. "Maybe a minute."

"Could you lie flat," he said, "I need to feel where your babies are."

Her abdomen was an enormous dome, the brown skin punctuated left and right with long pale diagonal stretch marks, her belly button everted and bulging. Pressing gently on Blossom's skin, Nick easily felt the heads of the twins, still breech, still headed out feet first.

"I'm going to do a quick exam inside," he told her. "First I need to go wash up." Mary followed him into the kitchen.

"No way she's in labor," Mary whispered.

"I know," Nick said, "But Wong'll ask about her cervix. I'm certain."

When Nick finished drying his hands, he had to ask Mary three times for a sterile glove and a dollop of lubricant. This was unexpected. It was their fourth case together, and the two had been evolving as a team, moving quietly through routines, anticipating the next thing, and the next. He'd witnessed that kind of special synchrony, particularly in the operating room between surgeons and scrub nurses, but he'd not experienced it himself. Medical students were transients, temporary beings, rotating here and then there, assigned to whomever for whatever. Discontinuity was their steady state. But these cases with Mary had been different. Something was off today, he thought. Something was wrong.

"She's maybe effaced a little," he said, his gloved and lubricated index and middle fingers feeling for the contours of the cervix. Stepping aside, he asked Mary what she thought.

"I'm gettin' one," Blossom said, "I'm gettin' one now." She'd been quiet and cooperative, seemingly still in thrall of Nick. "It's hurtin'."

He palpated her lower abdomen and could perceive no difference from minutes earlier. He turned to Carolyn, who was standing in the doorway of the bedroom. "How long would you say since the last one?"

"I'm not sure," Carolyn said, "maybe twenty minutes."

"And the one before that?"

"I don't know," she said, "but these don't seem like real labor pains to me. They just don't."

He pivoted back to Blossom. "You still got it?"

"Not as much. Maybe a little."

Without speaking, Nick gestured Mary to the foot of the bed. She snapped on a glove and executed a vaginal exam. "Well, she's not dilated at all," she said. "This isn't happening."

Nick invited Carolyn to the bedside and turned to his patient. "We don't think you're in labor, Blossom."

"These aren't labor pains?

"We're pretty sure they're not."

"Well, what are they?"

"We call it false labor," he said. "It happens a lot. Your uterus, your womb, it contracts, but not in a regular way, not in a way that moves your babies out."

"Are you sure?"

Nick glanced toward Mary, who turned away. He got the message. You're the doctor here.

"Yes Blossom," he said, "I'm sure."

As a senior medical student, he'd repeatedly experienced this disconnect—this gap between what he knew and what he was confident enough to stand behind. This was surely better than its opposite, better than ill-informed hubris.

He asked Caroline if he could use the telephone. He wanted to speak to Bill Wong, the resident on duty, but instead got Teresa Butler, who insisted that they stay with Blossom for a full eight hours before returning to the

Center. "That girl's too high risk to treat her as a routine 'false,'" Butler told him. "You stay with her, you re-examine her hourly. She blinks, you get her to County."

Nick had experienced long waits in two of his Maternity Center cases. A woman in Douglas Park had a very prolonged labor but eventually delivered a healthy newborn. In the breech case with Helen Jackson, they had to wait a good while for Westerman before moving ahead. This case felt different. They'd been in Caroline's apartment for less than two hours, but without the prospect of a delivery the wait felt interminable. Each glance at his wristwatch was a disappointment.

Blossom was napping, her nephews were in their bedroom watching TV and Caroline was busy in the kitchen. Alone in the living room, Nick and Mary sat quietly in their scrubs. He was on the couch with his stocking feet on the coffee table, she was directly opposite in an upholstered chair mechanically thumbing a magazine. He'd been thinking that she didn't seem herself. She was typically cheerful, occasionally sassy, always helpful. Today she was distracted. We're it not for the ocean of time on their hands, he'd have probably let it be.

"Are you all right?" he said. "You seem, I don't know, someplace else."

When Mary didn't respond, he figured he'd made a mistake. He thought she was silently letting him know that his question was too personal or that his judgment was unwelcome. He was surprised, then, at her transparency when she finally spoke up. "Today is the one year anniversary of my Nana's death," she said. "The woman was everything to me. I don't know where I'd be if it wasn't for her. Maybe an alcoholic like my mother, a junkie, a hooker, I don't know. That all seems possible. She saved me. Plain and simple, she saved me. I miss her every day."

Nick watched her open her purse, extract a tissue and dry her eyes. He was no therapist, but he understood that the one thing he had to offer was his attention. "Would you mind telling me about her?" he said. "What was she like?"

She hesitated again, a melancholy smile breaking at the corners of her mouth. "She was tough," Mary said. "More than anything, she was courageous. When I was in eighth grade these girls on our block would give me a hard time when I got off the bus from Catholic school. They'd call me names and push me around. One time they knocked me down and I cut my lip. I ran in the apartment bleeding and crying. Nana went out there with a rolling pin—and these were big girls, about five of them—and I remember what she said. She said, 'One of you touches my Mary again, I'm gonna crack your head open.' I'll never forget it.

"I can remember the day she took me away from my mother. I was only four, but I remember it. Maybe not every detail, but enough. Nana was telling my mother that she had to stop drinking. There was nothing unusual about that, but Nana was really upset that day, I don't know why. She left and came back with a bunch of shopping bags and told me to put all my clothes, all my things, in the paper bags, that we were leaving, that I was going home with her. My mother went crazy, screaming at her, throwing things.

She picked up a carving knife and was waving it around. Nana just stood her ground and marched me out of there. Left my mother crying on the kitchen floor. I was scared to death."

Mary was child-like, undefended, as she spoke. This was all the more touching to Nick, given how he admired her strength and competence. "Can you talk about some happy memories," he said, "some happy stories about her?"

She brightened as she reminisced about how they shopped together for her confirmation dress, went on the rollercoaster at Riverview Park, spent a weekend in Lake Geneva, saw a Sox game at Comisky. She said she'd never seen Nana happier than at her nursing school graduation. "She was all dressed up," Mary said, "holding a big bouquet of flowers. She told me that she was so proud of me, that I was her special prize. She liked to call me that, her special prize."

Now she was smiling and crying. Caroline interrupted, leaning into the living room. "Excuse me, would you all like some breakfast?"

When Caroline withdrew, Mary reached across the table and took Nick's hand in both of hers. "Thank you Nick."

"You're welcome, I guess, but I really didn't do anything."

"Yes, you did," Mary said. "You did."

The six of them were crowded around Caroline's rectangular kitchen table. Nick and Mary, side by side, across from

Caroline and Blossom, Charles and Richie on the ends. Blossom's pains had abated, and after a third negative exam Nick decided that it was all right for her to be out of bed. Two hours had passed, there were six to go.

"This is quite something," Nick said. "I take it this is not your routine breakfast." In the center of the table there was a mountain of steaming fried chicken, a platter of waffles, another of biscuits, and maple syrup and butter and honey and jams and pitchers of coffee, orange juice and milk.

Caroline had done this without fanfare. "You folks hungry?" she'd asked. "I'll put something together."

Richie, the four year-old with the exotic form of epilepsy, was to Nick's immediate left. It wasn't his intention to give the little boy a diagnostic once over, but seeing him, he couldn't help himself. The word that Nick's teachers had used to describe a countenance like Richie's was "moon-faced," round and puffy, characteristic of the long-term effect of steroids. Nick knew that Richie was likely receiving a hormone injection, a drug called ACTH, that was leading to his altered appearance. It was the treatment of choice for the boy's type of seizures.

Nick looked up to find Blossom watching him watch her nephew. "Time for some chicken," he said, uneasy, as if he'd been caught doing something wrong.

"So what do you think?" Blossom asked.

"I think this is a wonderful breakfast. It's really generous of Caroline—"

"No, no," she said, "what do you think about Richie?"

His impulse was to tell her, with authority, that this visit was for her and her babies and not for her nephew, and that her sister had gone through all this trouble, so let's just enjoy the meal. Instead, he turned to his reliable refuge of self-deprecation.

"You know, I'm not a pediatrician or a neurologist. I'm the last person you'd want giving you opinions about Richie. Really."

Blossom's disappointment was transparent, her eyes averted, her lips pursed.

He remembered her volatility in the examining room at the Center—from nearly catatonic withdrawal to excited engagement, and her sudden outburst of anger and her desperate dependency. He felt the weight of her fragility, that she might explode or collapse at any setback, large or small. He now held, through the accident of circumstance, far more power than he wanted over this teenager's emotional landscape.

Always uneasy with the discomfort of others and guilty as a matter of, well, breathing, he negotiated. "We'll be here a long time today," he said, "let's be sure to talk about Richie later."

Nick, the kid from a two-generation restaurant family and no pushover when it came to food, savored every bite of Caroline's home cooking. He'd heard stories about this, about the hospitality and generosity of Maternity Center patients and their families. Of gifts, which they weren't officially allowed to accept, and meals and transportation and protection. Some of the slum tenement visits would feel like family, he'd been told, and this one certainly did.

At meal's end, the boys were shooed away and Mary joined Caroline at the sink, washing and drying in newfound partnership. Nick, having helped clear the table, sat alone with Blossom, at a loss for how to conversationally fill these hours. There were five more to go. He killed a few minutes with a repeat examination of her cervix, which he knew was going to be unchanged, and there they were again at the kitchen table.

Sitting there, he had no expectation other than running out the clock, which felt like it was barely running at all. What a stupid policy, he thought, wasting time with a patient who was obviously not in labor.

He volunteered to talk with Blossom about Richie, and that consumed, at most, another five minutes. He told her that Richie looked better than most children with his diagnosis, which was true, and emphasized again that the child neurologist he was recommending would be able to give her far more information than he could. She lit up at Nick's 'looked better' observation and didn't press for more, as if 'more' would risk bad news after good.

It was Saturday morning and a cartoon show was blaring from behind the kitchen wall. *Speed of lightning, roar of thunder, Underdog, Underdog.* Caroline, otherwise soft-spoken, boomed her displeasure. "Charles, turn that damn thing down." *To right this wrong with blinding speed goes Underdog, Underdog.* "Charles, don't you make me come in there."

Nick and Blossom fell back into awkward silence. He was prospecting for something, anything, to talk about. Then Caroline saved him. "Blossom honey, why don't you show Doctor Nick your book."

Expecting at least reticence, he was surprised by

Blossom's enthusiasm, and more by the book itself. It was two feet long and a foot and a half high, with thick black cardboard covers front and back, and double wire binding for turning. She sat in the chair next to him and without speaking opened it. The pages were cream colored and thick, their tiny pressed wood fibers visible throughout. On the first was a pastel sketch, an exterior of a building, her building, in browns and oranges and black. Nick knew a bit about art, and this did not look like the work of a child.

"These are yours?" he asked. "You did these?"

"I did," she said, "go ahead, you turn the pages."

He moved slowly through the drawings, his surprise camouflaged as he recalibrated his conception of this fourteen year-old. There were a few more sketches of buildings, of street scenes, one that looked like nearby Garfield Park with its lagoon and flower conservatory, but most were portraits, and most of them were readily recognizable. The faces of Caroline, Charles and Richie were evoked by the curve of a cheekbone, the shape of a mouth, the character of a glance, something precise in its demeanor. Nick was impressed by her technique, which was spare, but even more by her eye, which seemed to easily set aside the extraneous, leaving intact the specific, the unique.

"These are wonderful," he said. "How long have you been doing this?"

"A long time," Blossom said. "Are you going to look at the rest?"

There were more drawings of the immediate family members, a few faces he didn't recognize and some additional neighborhood scenes. When he turned to the last drawing, it seemed out of place and at first he had little reaction, his attention numbed. Within a few seconds, though, he understood what he was looking at. The subject, a male, was dressed in loose-fitting pants and shirt, both green, and a white waist-length jacket. His skin was a medium shade, not obviously white or black, his hair dark and thick. There was a roughly drawn object around his neck which on closer inspection was a stethoscope. It was him, it was Nick, as he had appeared to Blossom in the clinic a few days earlier.

His throat tightened as he spoke. "This is really nice. I don't know what to say."

"Then you like it?"

"I like it very much," he said, "I'm just surprised."

She looked down at the drawing for several seconds. Then she gripped the cover with one hand and with the other carefully pulled the page away from its wire binding. "Here," she said, "so you won't forget me."

"Blossom, I'm not going to forget you."

"So you'll remember me and you'll keep your promise?" she asked. "You'll be with me when I'm in real labor, when I'm havin' these babies?"

He'd not yet taken the drawing from her, but when he did, a moment later, it felt like it sealed their covenant. His promise was no more sensible than it was in the first place, yet he could not bring himself to unmake it. He'd keep it if he could, but he knew that he would probably not be able to. He would be on another case or off the Maternity Center rotation entirely. But face to face, he didn't have the heart, or the courage, to tell this girl that she could not count on him.

When their time was finally up and they said their goodbyes, Blossom once again embraced him and he once again was speechless.

Nine Days Down

It was a lousy week for sports on television. Season openers for the Sox and Cubs were several days away and the Bulls had just been eliminated by the Lakers in the NBA semi's. Bobby Hull and the Blackhawks had made the Stanley Cup playoffs, but their quarter-finals against the Rangers hadn't yet begun. With the Bears deep in off-season hibernation, the TV was bereft of anything athletic, save bowling and wrestling.

Nick, who had scavenged two pieces of pizza and a taco from the barracks kitchen, switched channels from "Garrison's Gorillas" to "Daktari" to "I Dream of Jeannie" without a glimmer of interest. Last in the medical student queue after his long day with Blossom and well behind on sleep, he was content with an empty evening, no poker, the quieter the better.

He'd been in the Maternity Center rotation for nine days now, and the end was in sight. Wednesday through

Sunday, and then it would be over. Back to his own bed, his own food, his normal life, back to safety. And back to the future, his plans for internship and beyond. His path would not be inner-city, it would not be obstetrics, it would not in any way resemble what he was doing at the Maternity Center.

This experience, he thought, was reckless, and he didn't keep it to himself. Of the five medical students in the group, he was the most outspoken about both their medical un-preparedness and the danger of the neighborhoods. As the days wore on, though, his complaints dwindled, not because he changed his mind, but out of weariness. He was tired of complaining, and the others, he thought, we're tired of hearing him complain. Larry Berlin, the poker smart ass, was abrupt the day before, changing the subject in Nick's mid-sentence. Even Jeff, his only real friend in the group, remained mute the last time Nick recounted his anxious inventory.

He turned off the TV, stretched out on the brown cor-duroy sofa and began a drowsy encounter with a chapter from Topaz, an international suspense yarn by the author of Exodus, a novel he'd enjoyed in high school. A few min-utes in, at the edge of sleep, he was jarred by the clamor of stomping feet and conversation. Just inside the front door, Jeff and Jim Fisher liberated the snow from their boots as they shed the layers that insulated them from the bluster of the evening's unexpected storm.

"You're lucky to be inside," Jeff said, oblivious to the harshness of their interruption. Nick sat up, his nervous system getting its bearings. "And you're lucky you weren't up for this case."

He knew that there was no need to ask, that a tale was about to be told. This was how it went. The routine stuff was not fodder for discussion. But when there was anything out of the ordinary, each of the five would serve up an earful for the others, each description, for better or worse, expanding the collective experience.

"We just got back from Uptown," Jeff began, "a teenager with an unattended stillbirth. She said she was eighteen, but I don't know."

Nick knew all about the Uptown neighborhood. While it was not very far from Rogers Park, the middle class North Side enclave where he grew up, ethnically and culturally the Uptown might as well have been in another hemisphere. It was Little Appalachia—predominantly white and dirt poor. A magnet for unemployed Kentucky emigres, the Chicago newspapers referred to it as Hillbilly Heaven. Neglected in the extreme, there were more building fires in the Uptown than in any other neighborhood in Chicago.

"I doubt that girl's a day over sixteen," Fisher said. "And the father, I mean the guy who would have been the father, he looks like he coulda been forty. And he's pissed off and he's drunk and he's got these fucking weapons on the wall."

Now Nick was unequivocally awake. "Weapons on the wall?"

"Yeah, weapons," Jeff said. "Swords, guns, axes—"

"—and a big fucking confederate flag," Fisher added.

Nick kept his immediate response to himself, though a generous helping of 'I told you so' would have been gratifying. These are the guys who were not so subtly responding to him as if he were paranoid. He thought they were all in denial, whistling through this ghetto graveyard.

Jeff sat down in the easy chair opposite Nick and waded into the details. "It was called in as a stillbirth," he said. "We go up there to make sure the placenta's out and intact, and to make sure this girl—her name is Iris—to make sure Iris isn't bleeding. And as soon as we get there, this guy's in our face, screaming at us, blaming us for the stillbirth, blaming us for this dead baby."

Nick could see that Jeff was shook up. He'd known him for years, all the way back to pre-med downstate at the University of Illinois. Despite his response with the Abrafo and his freshman fainting episode, Jeff was typically the calmest of med students, the guy who kept his cool under pressure. He didn't sweat exams or formal presentations or medical emergencies. Before a particularly daunting freshman biochem final, Nick reached over and took Jeff's pulse. He told him that he just wanted to see if he had one.

Now Jeff was out of his chair, pacing as he spoke, the meter of his voice quickened, agitated. "This guy scared the crap out of me," he said. "He was way too close, with his fucking beer breath all over me. He's yelling that we should have known that something was wrong at Iris's last prenatal visit. And there was no calming him down. Everything we said just got him more pissed off. I really thought we were going to have to physically fight the guy."

"I was standing between him and his wall of weapons," Fisher said. "I thought any second he was gonna go for one of them and I was gonna have to try and stop him."

Nick wanted none of this. The two of them had obviously gotten out unharmed, and their fevered account was at this point little more than fuel for Nick's own anxiety. What he'd wanted was hours of nothing at all, and then sleep. Instead, he's sitting there ingesting one more helping of scared shitless. Metaphorically, his colon had been empty for days.

Jeff kept talking and Nick, in spite of his discomfort, was too well mannered to get up and walk away or tell his friend to shut up. Next came the clinical details, the hideous and heartbreaking appearance of the dead fetus and the placenta, and what felt like an interminable description of Iris, emptied and sullen.

Nick was drifting—exhausted, losing focus, his thoughts looping from Iris to Blossom and back again. This had to stop. Finally, Fisher described how the scary weapons guy backed off when they told him that they hoped they wouldn't have to call the police, and turned their full attention to Iris.

Fisher gave Nick an empty moment before his next sentence, whatever it might have been, and Nick took it. "I've had it, guys," he said, standing up. "I've got to get some sleep."

He'd been advised to bring an extra blanket from home, that the barracks bedrooms, with their tile floors and leaky windows, could be frigid, despite the calendar's assurance that it was springtime. The radiators steamed and clanked, but they were a poor match for Lake Michigan's icy windblown assault on a stormy night.

Nick was beneath two blankets, first the thin green military-looking one provided by the Center, and above that the all-wool Hudson Bay he'd been sleeping under for as long as he could remember. Like his mother's dark blue roasting pan with the white speckles, it seemed like every family he knew owned one of these. It was the classic creamy white blanket with green, red, yellow and black horizontal stripes, and heavy, but not oppressively heavy. It was reassuring, something from childhood, a guarantor of warmth, even of safety. It was just right. He was asleep, it seemed, in seconds.

He would remember only the worst of it, but his dream began in a peaceful place, a quiet nearly empty room with a table in the middle and one picture window. Through it he could see colorless irregular spaces between motionless clouds, more a black and white photograph than a living skyscape. The walls of the room were blank and there were no doors. He wondered for a moment how he got in there, and as quickly lost the thread of effect and cause, of time, of physics itself. It wasn't unpleasant yet. He was still an observer, a witness, scanning his strange enclosure.

The ceiling was as blank as the walls and indistinct in its connection to them. There was a gauzy blur where the surfaces should have met, and the corners of the room, top to bottom, looked the same, as if they were held together by something immaterial. After what might have been a long time, he looked around to find that the desk was no longer there, and there was a large weathered metallic object mounted where the window had been. It looked like the disfigured head of some kind of creature.

When the motion started, it was the ceiling slowly rising, its ethereal connector to the walls below stretching and thinning out. Then it paused and began its descent, first to where it started, and then lower. The pace was slow and at first was more fascinating than threatening. When the walls began to move toward one another, wonderment turned to fear, and then to terror.

The walls and ceiling rapidly closed in and then the floor began to rise. He was in an ever smaller box with each of the surrounding surfaces picking up speed. He elevated his arms to his sides, palms parallel to the oncoming walls. He could feel the force of his left ventricle slamming against the back of his breast bone, and hear the roar of air with each desperate breath. When the walls met his hands, he was helpless against their power, collapsing his wrists, elbows and shoulders.

I'm going to die right here, right now.

Within moments there was contact on every part of his body. As the floor and ceiling contracted, his head was forced to one side, his ear pressed into his shoulder, the upper part of his face against the ceiling. The force on his upper body compressed his lungs, each breath exhausting and possibly his last.

Then the motion stopped and briefly reversed, each surface withdrawing a small distance, just enough to breathe. The metallic object that had replaced the window was directly to his right, grotesque and almost touching his hip. Moments passed. There was a sound, like bubbling, and from an opening in the hideous head a liquid emerged, first in drops and then in a steady flow. He felt it on his feet and legs as its level ascended. When it reached his hands, it was thick, more like oil than water. When it reached his chest, he tried to scream. All the force he could muster produced not a sound. He screamed his silent scream again, and something, everything, changed.

This is impossible, he told himself, this cannot be real. The oily liquid was at his chin. Just try to relax. Any second I'll wake up and this'll be over. Now he was fully submerged in his liquid coffin. Ignore it, it can't hurt me, I'm dreaming, I'm dreaming. Suddenly the wall to his left slammed into him, striking his entire body, head to foot. He opened his undreaming eyes.

It took several moments for Nick to comprehend where he was. The first thing he saw was the floor beneath his bed. He'd fallen, landing on his left side, his blankets beneath him. His pajamas were soaked with sweat, his skin cold, his pulse and respirations as frenetic as they'd been in his hellish reverie. He was trembling. He rolled onto his back and tried to calm himself.

"I heard a crash. What happened?" It was Jeff. "Are you all right?"

"I fell out of bed. Do I look like I'm all right?"

"Here, let me help you up."

"That's all right. I just want to lay here and try and calm down. I had a really frightening dream and I just need to calm down." He wrapped the blankets around himself and closed his eyes.

Jeff sat on the edge of the bed and waited. After a few minutes he checked on his friend. "Nick?"

"Yeah."

"Can I do anything for you?

Several seconds passed and Jeff thought that he wasn't going to respond.

"Yeah," Nick finally said. "Can you get me the fuck out of here?"

April 4, Memphis

The New Rebel Motel was an ugly white one story trapezoid within earshot of the Memphis airport, a cock-eyed four-sided thing with guest parking in the big empty space in its misshapen middle. It was cheap and rundown and the surrounding area, southeast Memphis, was decayed and dangerous. It was Ray's kind of place.

He'd checked in late the night before as Eric S. Galt, his routine alias, and stayed up for hours drinking Schlitz and watching local news on television. He was annoyed at the attention given to a big weather story, a thunderstorm with tornado warnings that was washing through the city. The only thing he cared about was the reporting on Martin Luther King and the sanitation workers strike.

King was back in Memphis to lead another protest march and everyone including Ray knew where he was staying. The TV had it and so did the newspaper. Ray had gone out mid-morning to get another six-pack, a box of donuts and The Commercial Appeal, the morning daily. On the front page below the strike story there was a photo of King and three others on the balcony of the Lorraine Motel. They were standing near a door marked 306.

He found the motel's address in the telephone book, and using a city map spread out on the bed, zeroed in on the Lorraine's location. It was close to downtown, a half mile south of Beale Street and about the same distance from the Mississippi River to the west.

He'd been agitated for hours, sleep deprived and dirty and in no shape, he thought, to do what he wanted to do. First he cleaned the room, threw out the empties and half-eaten donuts, the cardboard containers. He folded up the map and neatly made the bed. Then he unpacked his dark gray suit, hand-pressed it the best that he could and placed it carefully on a hanger in the closet.

It took a while to get the hot water going in the shower. When it was ready he stepped in and took his time, slowing his breath, calming down. With his face immersed, eyes closed, he daydreamed his murderous intention. He believed that he had gotten this far, all the way from Jeff City, because he had vividly envisioned what he wanted to happen. Now, more than ever, he needed to do that. He imagined looking up at King, alone on that balcony, sighting through the crosshairs of the scope, finger on the trigger. You don't pull a trigger, his father had told him, you squeeze it. And in his waking dream he squeezed it.

Out of the shower, he shaved and dressed. He thought he looked respectable—white shirt and black tie, nice business suit, his glossy black dress loafers. A person who would pass muster, he thought, whatever kind of muster this day might require. He packed his things, put them in the trunk of the Mustang next to his rifle, and set out with no plan other than to find the Lorraine Motel and figure out some way to get to King. The map and front page photo were beside him on the front seat.

Angling up Lamar Avenue, backtracking the route he'd taken the night before, he dead-reckoned his way to Union, the east-west drag that spilled into the center of downtown. Past Sun Studio and the Peabody Hotel, he turned south onto Main Street and its trolley tracks and found a parking space on one of the small side streets that ran between Main and the river. Map in hand, he got out and strolled the neighborhood. He looked like a well-dressed tourist.

In less than five minutes Ray had his eyes on the motel's sign, a gaudy thirty foot high collage of pillars, marquee, logo and lettering in aqua, red, white and Crayola yellow. It caught his eye from three blocks away. Not wanting to be seen too close on foot, he returned to the Mustang and slowly cruised the streets encircling the motel. The west-facing balconies were easily seen. He couldn't make out the upstairs room numbers but one area of the balcony seemed to perfectly match the newspaper photo.

He circled the property again, this time focused not on the motel but on its surroundings. Opposite what he presumed was King's balcony were the rear windows of a two story brick building, slightly uphill, a few hundred feet away. It seemed to be the only structure with the sight lines that he was hoping for.

Perhaps it was his dressy attire, or the cold geometry

of the problem he was facing, but Ray was not roiling over King or 'the niggers' or any of that. He was clear-headed and clean and on a mission. Edging slowly up South Main, he found the front entrances of the building whose rear windows were facing the motel. There were three doors, one to a company specializing in amusement park rides, another to a dry goods firm, and a third door, between the other two, with a sign hanging above it. It read "APARTMENTS ROOMS." Ray backed the Mustang into an empty lot that bordered the south side of the building, He tucked it close to the brick wall, its front bumper as far forward as possible to the street. It was the way he always parked, poised for the quickest departure.

Inside, a sign directed him to a second story office. He knocked, and a short, fortyish brown-haired woman emerged into the hallway. He told her that his name was John Willard and that he needed a room. "I need it for a week," he said. "What do you charge?"

"I've got two I can show you," she answered, stepping around him. She led him down a hallway and opened the door to room 8. "This one's $12.50 for the week."

Looking in, Ray saw that it was a kitchenette and that its window faced west, away from the Lorraine. "I don't need the stove and the refrigerator, I just need a sleeping room."

He trailed her to 5B, a room on the opposite side of the hallway. "Is this to your liking? It's $8.50 for the week."

A quick glance verified that through its dirty window, through a cluster of tree branches, there was the Lorraine and its balconies. "This'll do," he said.

He was out on Main Street again, this time on foot, walking north toward the center of downtown. The area was historic—the palatial Orpheum Theater, Cotton Row, the Peabody Hotel where Jefferson Davis had lived, Beale Street with its bars and blues joints and Loew's State Theater, where 20 years earlier Elvis Presley got his first job as an usher. It was also the first job from which Elvis was fired. The story goes that he coldcocked a fellow usher with a right cross, thereby short-circuiting that particular career path.

Focused on finding a store where he could buy a pair of binoculars, Ray was oblivious to the glitz of Memphis. In his first minutes alone in the rooming house, he'd realized that surveillance of the Lorraine Motel would require more than the scope on his thirty-aught-six with its limited field of vision. He wanted to be able to have magnified vision of the whole balcony at once.

On the east side of Main, next door to Loew's Theater, the big display windows of the York Arms Sporting Goods store were loaded with mostly hunting gear, including a cluster of binoculars. Inside, the place looked as much like a museum as a retail shop, with its dark wooden floors, display cases, and the walls covered with animal heads and vintage weapons.

Ray found an array of dozens of binoculars, tried a few, and settled on a pair of Bushnell Banner 7 x 35's. The man behind the counter told him that these would magnify up to seven times and were good in low light. He paid in small bills, requested two extra dollars in change and asked the man if there was a pay phone nearby.

He was going to call his brother John, the only person in the world who knew what he was up to. John Larry Ray was, like his brother, a career criminal and an ex-con. Though he was five years younger, he was James' advisor and cheerleader. He'd told him which rifle to buy, which ammunition to choose. He was there a year earlier to drive him out of the countryside when he broke out of the Missouri State Penitentiary.

These two were raised in a household steeped in poverty and alcoholism, and under the hateful influence of the local Klan. Their father, George "Speedy" Ray, was a small-time hoodlum who moved the family from town to town avoiding the law, often changing names along the way—they were the Rayns at one point. Two of James and John's siblings didn't make it to adulthood—sister Marjorie dying in a house fire at age eight and brother Franklin drowning at 19.

They'd both been wild kids, but James was the more troubled, a bed-wetting stutterer with recurrent nightmares and violent anti-social behavior. He was unkempt and unpopular at school. One teacher, in a disciplinary report, wrote that he was repulsive.

At age 20 John went to prison for seven years for auto theft. He was arrested in a stolen Hudson, joy riding through the streets of Quincy, Illinois. When he got out, he settled in South St. Louis, where he eventually opened a downscale bar called the Grapevine Tavern. His big brother had the phone number of the place in the inside pocket of his suit jacket as he stepped into a phone booth on the sidewalk in front of the Orpheum Theater.

"Where the hell are ya?" John said.

"I'm in Memphis."

"Memphis? I thought you were in Atlanta. What the fuck are you doin' in Memphis?"

"You don't watch the news, do ya?"

John didn't watch the news, but he knew there could be only one reason that his big brother left Georgia for Tennessee. "He's there, is he?"

"He is."

"Jesus, can you get to him?"

"Looks like I can, maybe."

"Can I do something?" John said. "Anything you want me to do?"

"Maybe at some point. I might need some money, but right now…"

He recoiled in mid-sentence at the distraction of the conversation. He'd wanted to briefly check in and nothing more. John would just keep talking if he let him. He was focused on what was right in front of him, he was in that zone of intention that he knew he needed, that had gotten him this far.

"Look, Johnny, all goes well, soon it'll be over," James Earl Ray said. "I might not see you for a while, but don't worry about me. I'll be all right."

Barron's

Nick was bone tired, which was nothing new, but his nightmare had been depleting beyond the loss of sleep. He met the morning feeling endangered, that any awful thing was possible. When he learned that he was fourth in the queue for deliveries, that it would likely be several hours before his next case, it felt like a reprieve. Maybe he'd get a break, an easy Thursday.

Desperate to get away from the Center, he convinced Ernie to drive to Barron's for breakfast. The two of them were at a back table at the Roosevelt Road deli that Nick's grandparents had operated for almost forty years. Looking up from the menu, Nick asked Ernie what he was having.

"Lox and bagels," the big man said.

"Really?"

"I love Jewish food."

"Me too," Nick said, "I just hope it's as good as it used to be."

It had been eight years since Abe and Ruth Barron let go of their lifelong business. They sold the place to a Greek gentleman, a non-observant Jew from Athens who'd done well with a gyro enterprise on Maxwell Street. He kept the name and some of the menu, which was now a hodgepodge of traditional Jewish fare, Greek specialties and soul food—from chopped liver and matzo ball soup to souvlaki and dolmades to pork ribs and greens.

Barron's looked pretty much like it looked when Nick was a little kid. The cashier was near the door behind a big glass display of cigarettes and cigars. There was a gauntlet of take-out, case after case of meats and cheeses, smoked fish and herrings, salads and soups, cakes and cookies and pies. Behind the cases there were still some hanging salamis, which were now accompanied by the suspended quarters of animals that would have been decidedly off-limits ten years earlier. The parquet floor eventually made its way to the seating area, maroon booths and dark wooden tables and chairs filling the full width of the back half of the deli.

Celebrity photographs lined the walls, publicity shots with personal salutations to Abe and Ruth in bold script. The new owner kept these on display, promising he'd return them if he ever took them down. For decades, Jewish entertainers who traveled to Chicago made their way to Barron's for a hot corned beef sandwich or a plate of Ruth's brisket, and Abe never failed to get an autographed photo. Eddie Cantor even signed one to Nick, and so did Judy Holliday.

This had been a place of comfort for Nick. His *zayde* and *bubbe*, Abe and Ruth, were unsentimental survivors, hardened from the anti-Semitism of Europe and their bootstraps struggle to make it in America. They were no-nonsense at business and with their daughters, but relentlessly warm and generous with the *kinder*, the grandchildren.

When Nick was in sixth and seventh grade, before he was aswirl in the obsessions of puberty, he loved spending Saturdays at the deli. Abe would pick him up in his black Caddy for the half hour drive from West Rogers Park to Roosevelt Road. Nick especially liked it when Ruth stayed behind. He loved his *bubbe* but there was something wonderful about getting to sit in that big front seat and having Abe all to himself.

They had their rituals. Abe always offered Nick a cup of coffee. "Don't tell your mother," he'd say. Side by side they'd squeeze the rye breads to make sure they were fresh. And he'd have Nick count the cash from the previous day's business and write down the total, then Abe would count it and they'd compare.

Abe did this one particular thing, and always in the same way. He'd put his right hand in his pants pocket, look up at the ceiling, and move his hand around like he was searching for something. Finally the hand emerged with a shiny silver dollar held between his thumb and index finger. He'd hand it to Nick and say, "Now you save this, *boychek.*" Always, exactly like that. And save them he did. Nick still had dozens of them. He kept them in an old cigar box and most of the time had one on him for good luck.

There was a special table at lunch time on Saturdays, as many as seven or eight men including Abe, who made sure his grandson was at his side. "You sit right here, Nicky. You'll learn something."

And learn he did. Nobody else in his life talked like these men, certainly not his father. They talked about politics and economics, religion and ethics. They argued, but not like his family argued. They spoke in whole sentences and they didn't interrupt. They spoke of Senator Joe McCarthy, who was finally being rebuffed by the American public. They talked about Richard Daley, the ambitious Democratic Party operator and brand new mayor of the city. They spoke of big things—the Supreme Court banning segregation in the schools, the Warsaw Pact, Israel and the Palestinians. They were Democrats, every one of them, but they liked Eisenhower anyway.

The conversations were in one way or another about right and wrong. Abe told him, "Nicky, you have to have a moral compass." Nick thought the words were strange, the first time he heard them. Then for years he thought his *zayde* had invented them. He'd never heard anyone else say them. "You've got to know which way is north," Abe would say, "you've got to have a moral compass."

Abe's moral compass was about fairness. He revered F.D.R., whose programs had elevated the elderly and the working man. His idol in the 1950's was Walter Reuther, the Michigan-born union leader who successfully took on the U.S. automakers over pay and benefits for the workers. Abe called underpaid workers "wage slaves," which was one of Reuther's rallying cries. And Abe was outspoken about prejudice and the plight of minorities. He was well aware that there was tension on the West Side between the Jews and the Blacks, as often as not between slumlords and tenants, "but just remember," he said to Nicky, "the two groups have a lot in common, our enemies for example."

Nick was looking beyond Ernie's broad left shoulder at a photograph of Abe and Ben Turpin, the wacky cross-eyed silent film star, when the waitress came to take their order. She stood next to Nick, almost touching him, as he asked for a plate of potato latkes with apple sauce, a taste of childhood. "And you?" she said, neither moving toward nor looking at Ernie. When she returned a few minutes later with their food, she again positioned herself next to Nick, avoiding contact with the big and very black Maternity Center custodian.

Perhaps it was because Ernie had rescued him from the Abrafo a few days earlier, or maybe it was the conscience of *zayde* Abe inhabiting the place, but Nick could not abide what he just witnessed.

"That bother you?" he asked.

"Did what bother me?" Ernie said, painting a bagel with a generous glob of cream cheese.

"That waitress, she treated you like you were invisible, like you weren't even here."

Ernie put his knife down and paused, as if he were deciding whether this was a topic that he wanted to talk about with a young white man that he barely knew.

"Look doc," he finally said, "people been slavin' us, lynchin' us, treatin' us like disposable garbage for three hundred years. I grew up in Jim Crow north Florida, where, short of ownership, it might as well have been 1860. You think I'm gonna be upset at some frightened white lady who doesn't want to socialize with me?"

"Still," Nick said, "It's not right."

"Of course it's not right. Look, I don't have it nearly as bad as most of my brothers and sisters. Because of my size, the way I look, they don't fuck with me, they don't take me straight on. Nobody niggers me or spades me or coons me. That's not how it is. It's more like this waitress, who out of fear or hate or just plain stupidity can't even look at me."

Nick felt oddly honored at Ernie's choice to confide in him. At the same time, he was uncomfortable, thinking he'd impulsively waded into territory where he didn't belong. An olive-skinned kinky-haired Jew, he knew something about prejudice, but his mistreatment had been playground stuff, teasing untethered to violence. These people had been treated as subhuman, undeserving of respect, even of life itself. Sure, the Jews had been persecuted and butchered, but Nick had had no personal experience of that kind of murderous hatred.

His discomfort must have been evident. "Hey man," Ernie said, "am I making you nervous? Consider this part of your education. When it comes to race, I'll tell you all the truth you can handle."

Ernie was smiling, and Nick got his nerve up. "Okay, what's it like to be a black man in a white man's world?"

"Now there you go," Ernie said, "Now you're talkin'. First of all, I have no idea what it's like to be a black man in a white man's world. I can't speak for anyone else. Just because we're in the same race, I don't know what someone else is feeling or assume that they feel what I feel. I can tell you what it's like to be me in this white man's world, I can do that.

"Okay," Nick said, "fair enough."

"Imagine that you, a grown man, have just said something to someone using a complete sentence, you know, a noun and a verb and all that shit, and they say, 'you are very well-spoken,' as if it's a compliment. They not only leave off the '...for a nigger' part, but they are truly unaware that that's what they're doing. Could you imagine being complimented for speaking as well as an eight year-old? Think about it.

"You're walking down the street and the woman walking toward you moves as far to the side as possible to get away from you, shifts her purse to that side and clutches it so hard you can see her white knuckles. By the way, the sisters do that too. Or worse, the woman or a guy or a couple cross the street so they don't have to pass you at all."

"I've done that," Nick confessed.

"Or just try to get a cab. I ain't had a taxi stop to pick me up in years. I don't even try any more. And for me, the worst thing is getting followed around like I'm a criminal. Imagine being shadowed in stores—Field's, Carson's, any of them. Uniformed security guards or plain clothes guys with bulges in their jackets following you around, assuming you're gonna steal something. This is not unusual, doc. This is day to day shit."

Nick wasn't surprised by any of it. He'd had these reactions himself, dished out the insulting compliments. He struggled for a response and all he could muster was "I understand."

"Okay," Ernie said, "now it's your turn."

"My turn?"

"Yeah, your turn. Your turn to speak some truth."

"You mean, what's it like to be a white man in a white man's world?"

"Very funny," Ernie said. "No, some truth, tell me some truth. Tell me why you're so fuckin' scared of us."

"You really want me to try to talk about that?"

"Yeah, I do."

Nick's brain stood still. "You want to give me a minute?"

"Take all the time you want," Ernie said, returning to the adornment of his bagel.

As he began to harvest his thoughts, Nick understood that he had both the burden and the luxury to set bullshit aside and speak truthfully about something important and hard. Ernie's honesty and invitational directness had made it so. This was an unrecognizable moment, and he had no choice but to have it.

"You know, there were some tough white guys in my high school," Nick began. "About half the school was Jewish, and the other half was a mixture of a bunch of different groups, only a few black kids though. There were some tough Jewish guys, but the toughest guys were the Irish guys. They really liked to fight. They'd pick fights all the time, usually after school.

"Two guys would square off and a crowd would form around them. They'd start off boxing and then it would turn into a punching wrestling brawl until one of them gave up or got a bloody nose or something. If it looked like one of them was really in trouble, the crowd would pull them apart. That was it. There were no weapons. They weren't trying to kill each other. You might get a black eye or a lose a tooth, but that was about as bad as it got."

Nick hesitated. There was nothing he could discern from Ernie, who was placidly devouring his bagel. "I believe, and I know I'm not alone in this, that if I got into it with someone in this neighborhood, especially with a gang member, I could very well end up stabbed or shot. Possibly dead. I don't think that's paranoid, I think that's reality."

"You Northwestern boys been coming here something like 70 years now," Ernie said. "Anybody been killed?"

"There've been muggings, just happened last week to Bobby Plunkett."

"Did he get hit, kicked, shot, stabbed?"

"Well, no," Nick said. "Still, you can't tell me that this isn't a dangerous place. Those Abrafo guys are dangerous and you know it. Christ, you were there. If you weren't, I don't know what would have happened."

Ernie set his bagel on its plate, folded his arms across his chest and placidly waited.

"Look, we've been told our whole lives, by everyone around us, that you people were predators, that you had knives and guns, that you hated whites, that we would be crazy to go into your neighborhoods. Maybe we didn't use the word 'nigger,' but you were 'the coloreds' or 'the *schvartzes*,' and the meaning was the same. We grew up hearing nothing but denigration and warnings. Sure, we support your causes, civil rights and voting rights, but we don't want you near us. What did Dick Gregory say? We don't care how big you get, as long as you don't get close."

"Hey," Ernie said, "I ain't questioning whether you're scared. Everybody knows you're scared. Everybody knows you think we're dangerous. I'm asking why that is, why you all think we're so fuckin' dangerous."

Now Nick was fidgeting with his food, rearranging the lox, tomato and onion on his half-eaten poppy seed bagel. "I don't know," Nick said, "probably because we've treated you like shit for centuries and in many ways we still treat you like shit, and you despise us for it. And we think that you're physically stronger than us, that you could overpower us."

Ernie watched Nick return to his breakfast. "So we're pissed off and some of us are strong," Ernie said. "Doesn't necessarily mean we're going to do something about it. You got any other thoughts?"

Nick had gotten his courage up and waded further into the conversation than he could have imagined. Now he was emptied out and growing apprehensive, his body wanting to get out of the chair. It wasn't Ernie making him nervous, it was the seconds of silence, the dead air. The big man sat there like a benign Buddha, looking like he could be comfortable in the quiet for days.

Nick couldn't tolerate it. "I just don't know what you want me to say."

Ernie made him wait a few moments longer before completing his kind and ruthless tutorial, before leaving nothing on the bone. "How about you think we can't control ourselves, that we're primitives, wild animals. And what's more dangerous than an angry wild animal."

"I wouldn't say that," Nick said. "I can't say that."

"I know you can't."

Baseball Weather

You don't kick the snow in Chicago. It snows and then it freezing rains and then they salt it, and then it snows again, and it goes on like that until you have these encrustations, these hard-as-a-brick urban moguls of ice and salt and tire churn, toe breakers. It was April fourth and glops of the stuff like arctic pseudopods were still keeping a scattered clutch of the sidewalks, making their last stand in the face of baseball weather. The sun was out and so were people on Maxwell Street.

Back from Barron's, Nick was disappointed. Upon arrival, he was first in the queue for deliveries and within minutes he was out again, accompanied by a nursing student he'd not met, one not nearly as comely as the distracting Kathy-with-a-K. It was labeled an uncomplicated case, a multip with good prenatal care who'd gone into labor at term, right on schedule.

The patient's tenement was larger than most, four

stories with a double-entrance to sixteen apartments almost directly across the street from the Maternity Center. Walking in, Nick realized that he'd been there before. This was the building where he, with an assist from Teresa Butler, had delivered Freddie, the sister of Sonny the Abrafo gang member.

Up two flights, the apartment was homey, a well-kept place with family photos and an overflowing bookcase against the living room wall. He and his nursing student, her name was Maria, were escorted in by a young black man in dark slacks, a white dress shirt and black tie. He was about Nick's age and had a formal air about him, his erect posture and carefully enunciated speech. "I'm Deacon Brown," he said, "Elizabeth's brother."

Elizabeth was their patient, a 27 year-old with two preschool children, neither of whom were in evidence. Nick introduced himself and Maria to Mr. Brown and was about to ask to see Elizabeth when the young man said, "May I ask, sir, are you a religious person?" Given the purpose of the visit, this was a thought-stopping question.

"What?"

"I asked if you were a religious person?"

"Uh, not particularly, but why would you ask me that?"

"How about you, miss. Are you a religious person?"

"Yes, I am," Maria said. "I'm Roman Catholic."

"I see. Well, would the two of you mind if I say a prayer for the occasion?"

On first sight, Nick had wondered if the young man, given his attire and bearing, was a Black Muslim. He'd delivered a baby in a Nation of Islam family and the adult males were dressed like Mister Brown. "Sure, I guess," Nick said, thinking that Allah was about to be invoked.

"Lord God," Deacon Brown began, "you made us out of nothing and redeemed us by the precious blood of your only son. Preserve the work of your hands, and defend both Elizabeth and the tender fruit of her womb from all perils and evils. I beg of you, for Elizabeth, your grace, protection, and a happy delivery. Sanctify her child, and make this child yours forever. Grant this through Christ our Lord. Amen."

Maria amen'ed, Nick did not.

They found Elizabeth, who appeared to be asleep, in the bedroom beneath a large crucifix on the wall. Nick let her be for the moment, while he strolled the apartment looking for the best place to set up. He knew what he was looking for—a table large and high enough to work for the delivery, a few side tables for instruments and supplies, and ready access to hot water. He decided on the dining room, which was adjacent to the kitchen and had the surfaces he needed. He asked Maria to unpack the routine instruments and elicited the brother's aid in positioning the furniture.

Nick moved through the preparations with decisiveness. Despite his desire to just get this whole Maternity Center business over with, he was feeling more comfortable with the role and more adept at the technical tasks, at least in the uncomplicated cases. Yes, he wanted out, but he was not exactly the medical student that he was ten days earlier. He was becoming a bit more competent, even confident.

He heard Elizabeth call out from the bedroom. They found her sitting up in bed, placid, a pretty and well-kept young woman, defying Nick's expectation of the haggard ghetto multip to whom he'd become accustomed. "I just finished a contraction," she said. "They're about three minutes apart now."

"Let's have a look," Nick said, gesturing to Maria for assistance. Waiting for gloves and lubricant, he rushed through the introductions and a few questions—when did her pains began, had her water broken, was there bleeding, the usual. Everything pointed to an uneventful labor.

He examined her on the bed and immediately knew that there was little time to waste. "She's fully dilated. Let's move her right now." With the help of her brother they got her quickly up onto the dining room table, which Maria had covered with newspaper.

When everything was ready, this was the most orderly and least dramatic obstetrical situation he'd been in since arriving at the Maternity Center. Elizabeth was stoic, quietly breathing through her contractions, peacefully surrendering to her caretaking strangers. Maria, to Nick's left, had that surgical nurse's knack of keen observation and timing, each instrument and supply served up just when it was needed. The Deacon had positioned himself in a far corner behind his sister, out of eyeshot of her exposed anatomy, an open dog-eared bible in hand.

Nick was in a rare state. He was in command and comfortable. His anxiety, as ever-present as gravity, was at bay. He was nervous and confident anyway, standing calmly alongside his fear. He was even aware that the moment was fragile.

"Let me know when you feel like you need to push," he told Elizabeth. "You don't need to force it, you'll know and we'll help you."

Between contractions, he gave her a local anesthetic injection in case he needed to do an episiotomy. He had no intention, though, of doing a regional block. If the labor became prolonged and difficult, help was right across the street and he wouldn't hesitate to ask.

"Ooh, this is a hard one," Elizabeth said, the tension around her mouth and her eyes revealing more than her words.

"Children are a gift from the Lord, they are a reward from him…"

It was spoken softly, but it was startling. Nick knew that the Deacon was holding a bible, but he didn't expect him to begin quoting scripture aloud during the delivery. At the same time, he couldn't think of a sound reason to object.

"Is that okay?" he asked Elizabeth.

"Is what okay?"

"The bible verses, your brother reading bible verses."

"Well, of course that's okay," she said, apparently bewildered that anyone would ask such a thing.

Nick glanced at Maria to gauge her reaction, but she was head down, making herself busy rearranging the instruments.

Over the next several minutes, the contractions both quickened and increased in force, and judging by Elizabeth's moaning, had become much more painful.

"Anyone who welcomes a little child like this on my behalf welcomes me…"

"Elizabeth, let's try pushing with the next one, okay?"

Her face and chest were now covered with a thin layer

of sweat and she was breathing hard, even though the last contraction had finished. "Yeah, okay," she said.

Nick quietly told Maria to have the scissors ready in case he needed to do an episiotomy. "I don't think I'll need to," he said, "but just in case."

"Okay, I'm gettin' one," Elizabeth said. "Oh, sweet Jesus."

"All right, now push," Nick said. "Really push, push as hard as you can."

The head was crowning, a dome of wet and matted black hair pushing the labia apart. This is maybe going too fast, Nick thought. "Okay, stop pushing," he said. "Let's wait for the next one and bring your baby out nice and easy."

"Every good gift and every perfect gift is from above, coming down from the father of lights…"

And one more push and that was it. Nick had a wet and slippery baby girl in his hands. He pivoted to Maria who placed two clamps across the umbilical cord and cut between them with the scissors. They were almost done.

The Deacon had stepped forward and was stroking the sweat off of his sister's face and forehead. "Thank you," he said to Nick, "it's a sacrament, you know, the thread of creation."

Nick looked up from his final task, the delivery of the afterbirth, and acknowledged the Deacon with a nod and a tenuous smile. From what little this Jew knew about Christianity, it was baptism, and not childbirth, that was a sacrament, but he was not going to wade into those waters.

He tugged patiently on Elizabeth's end of the umbilical cord, trusting that the placenta would fully separate from the uterus and make its way out. In his limited experience, it always did. Standing there waiting, he realized that there were crucifixes on all four walls of the dining room. He was thinking that he'd had just about enough Jesus for one afternoon.

His principal conversation with himself, though, was about his professional performance. This was the smoothest delivery of his young career and perhaps his best moment as a clinician in any of his medical school rotations. And he did it without an intern or a resident or an attending physician.

The placenta eased out cleanly and it was time to get out of there. He quickly examined the baby as Maria gave follow-up instructions to the mother. After the gratitudes and goodbyes, the Deacon handed him a sealed white envelope. "This is a contribution to the Maternity Center," he said, "for what you did for Elizabeth and what you people do for this community. God bless you."

Nick stepped out of the tenement feeling buoyant, and in the time it took for the door to close behind him his sense of well-being evaporated into dread.

First he saw the long leather jackets, six of them. The young men were clustered around a black four-door Lincoln convertible parked at the curb with its top down. One of them was in the driver's seat, slouched under a black White Sox cap, his left arm draped over the steering wheel. The others were leaning against the car, three with their backs turned and two directly facing Nick, their unmistakable logos on display.

"Just walk," he whispered to Maria, who was to his right. They were each carrying a large leather equipment bag. He could feel his heart, its pulse transmitted into his throat.

"Hey whatcha got there?"

"It's our medical equipment," Nick said, still walking. "We're from the Maternity Center. We just delivered a baby here."

"Hey, hold on. I got some questions for you."

He didn't recognize the questioner. He was afroed like the others, and tall. His mind racing, Nick thought that the more of them the better, the less likely one of them would do something. He whispered to Maria again, "Just keep going."

"Hey stop. Don't you walk away when I'm talking to you."

"Leave them alone," Nick heard one of the others say. "They didn't do nothin'."

"Bullshit," the first one said, "they're disrespecting me."

"Yeah, well," a third voice said, "you don't deserve no fuckin' respect."

This got a laugh from the group and Nick kept walking, nervous still, but now thinking that perhaps nothing was going to happen.

"Stop! Don't you take another fucking step." This was a fourth voice, and it was followed by silence. No laughter, no wisecracks, nothing. Nick stopped and waited, his back to the Abrafo, Maria following his lead.

"Turn around."

Nick slowly pivoted.

"You and I are gonna have a little talk." The voice of authority was the one behind the wheel. He stepped out of the convertible and said to Maria, "You get outta here, you just go." Nick nodded his assent and she headed across the street toward the Maternity Center.

It took Nick several seconds to focus, to comprehend who this was. The Sox cap, an upturned collar, aviator shades, together serving as camouflage, hiding the young man behind his paraphernalia of cool. But then he got it. It was Sonny.

He'd been both menacing and tender at his sister Freddie's delivery, but now he was scarily one-dimensional as he walked toward Nick. It was clear that he was at the top of the pecking order of this cluster of gang members, and that he alone would dictate what was about to happen.

"You remember me?" Sonny asked.

"Of course," Nick said, "You're Freddie's brother, the uncle of the little girl we delivered here."

"Because I know we all look alike, I figured maybe you couldn't tell one of us from the other."

"No, I recognized you." Nick said it quietly, adopting as friendly a presence as he could muster.

Sonny let several seconds pass and then he spoke as softly as Nick, barely above a whisper. "I suppose you think that you'll get a pass because of what you did for my sister. And maybe you should. I'd be a real bastard not to show you some appreciation. Ain't that right?"

Nick was at a loss for where this was going. Fighting his way out of it was insane. He wouldn't last ten seconds. And there was no answering Sonny's questions, which weren't questions anyway.

"I just don't understand why you have a quarrel with us," Nick said. "We come here to learn, it's true, but we're here to help. You know that as well as anyone. You saw it for yourself."

"You don't understand why we have a quarrel with you," Sonny said. "You know, I believe that, that you don't understand. Maybe you need a history lesson. Maybe that'd help, but I ain't got the time or the desire to give you one."

Nick started to answer, and changed his mind. Sonny was going to do whatever he was going to do. There'd be no talking him into or out of anything. And there'd be no rescue. The cops weren't around and Ernie wasn't coming. Nick would keep his mouth shut and just hope that Sonny would back off.

The two of them stood there, neither of them speaking, for what seemed to Nick a very long time. "Here's the thing," Sonny finally said, "and I feel bad about this, I really do. But I have a rep to keep up. I just can't afford to look soft in front of my boys. Do you understand?"

Nick understood all right, that he was about to get hurt. He just didn't know how and how badly. He began to step slowly backward. "Look," he said, "You don't have to do this. I've seen the other side of you and you do not have to do this. And what will you be proving anyway, that—"

"—I'll be proving whatever I fuckin' need to prove. You don't know this life. You come down here like you're on some kind of fuckin' field trip. You're gonna take care of us natives, right?"

"That's not fair at all," Nick said.

Suddenly there was the shock of Sonny's left hand hitting Nick's upper chest as he grabbed a fistful of his jacket. Nick was pulled up onto his toes within a few inches of the bigger man's face.

"Now here's what's going to happen," Sonny said. "You're going to go down and stay down. You don't even try to get up until I'm back in the car. Do you understand?"

As Nick started to answer, Sonny's right fist exploded into his midsection. His lungs emptied, and as he sprawled backwards onto the sidewalk, his solar plexus, the nerve center of his diaphragm, sent that huge indispensable muscle into paralytic spasm. For several seconds there was, despite every desperate effort, not a breath's worth of air refilling his airway. He was the luckless fish on the floor of the boat, gills flapping, suffocating.

He lay flat on the concrete until his breath returned, and then for a while longer, lingering under the blue baseball sky and thinking of nothing other than going home.

Above the Balcony

Ray sat in his parked Mustang waiting for a break in the traffic on South Main Street. The Remington rifle was in the trunk, in the box it came in and wrapped in an old green bedspread. Carried in his arms, its identification would not be obvious. Still, he wanted to be unseen walking it into the rooming house, twenty yards away.

"Do the thing and you will have the power," he said to himself, barely above a whisper. Then he said it again, and again. It was his mantra. During his time in Los Angeles, he became obsessed with psycho-cybernetics, a fringe psychology that preached single-minded action as the secret to success in all aspects of life. The words, co-opted from Emerson, served as shorthand for its philosophy.

"Do the thing and you will have the power." It had become a tic, echoing in Ray's brain, escaping his lips. Watching the cars and trolleys left and right, he kept it up. When the street was empty in both directions, he got out and opened the trunk, quickly retrieving the rifle and the bin-oculars. He made it to the front door of the rooming house and upstairs to room 5B without reason to believe that he'd been noticed. It was a few minutes past 5 p.m.

Inside, he rearranged the room, moving a rickety dresser away from the window, replacing it with a straight-backed wooden chair. He closed the flimsy cloth drapes, leaving a space between, wide enough to watch the motel. Using a pillow case, he was able to clean most of the dirt off the window.

He'd decided earlier, before he ventured out for the binoculars, that 5B would be good for surveillance, but not as good for shooting. If he got the opportunity, if King showed himself, he would fire the rifle from the bathroom just down the hall, where there was a more promising line of sight and where he would be better concealed.

He'd gotten himself within striking distance of his prey with a weapon that could do the job. Now all he could do was wait. He sat down in the chair and scanned the mo-tel through the Bushnell's. He would need to be patient. He could be there for hours or days. He could be there for nothing.

Ray was twitchy and restless in ordinary moments, a be-ing whose nervous system was in relentless low-level vibra-tion. He'd tried yoga and meditation. His compulsive mas-turbation was as sedative as it was sexual and kinky. Now he was wired, barely able to remain in his chair—sitting briefly, getting up and pacing, sitting again, his eyes fixed through the binoculars on the door to Room 306 across the way. He forced himself to slow his breath, counting to ten between each cycle. "Do the thing and you will have the power. Do the thing...."

Room 5B was a dump, even worse than his usual choice of lodging. The paint was chipped and peeling from the wood trim around the windows, the wallpaper separating from the walls. A portion of ceiling plaster was gone, exposing rotted lath. The wooden floor was cracked and uneven. A bare light bulb hung from the center of the ceiling, a dirty white string dangling from it. The hall bathroom was filthy, the sink coated with soap scum, the toilet streaked, the claw foot bathtub likewise coated, its drain clogged with hair, the linoleum floor buckled and stained. The whole area— the sleeping room, the hallway, the bathroom—smelled like piss.

Ray was inured to crappy surroundings. They'd been a constant since Jeff City. Every molecule of his awareness was focused on what he could see through the window— a downhill threadbare slope strewn with trash, a low retaining wall, then Mulberry Street, which was barely more than an alley, and then the motel itself, 50's-era dull yellow cinder block with turquoise trim. The door to Room 306 was roughly two hundred feet away and twelve feet below Ray's position. It led onto a balcony with a painted steel railing which overlooked a parking area below, its pavement puddled from the previous evening's heavy rain. Through the binoculars, which had the same 7x magnification as the scope on his rifle, the numbers on the motel door looked like they were ten yards away.

He'd leaned the rifle, still in its box and wrapped in the green bedspread, upright against the wall in the sleeping room close to the door. If King appeared—at the door to 306, on the balcony, on the outside stairway, in the parking lot—Ray would grab the rifle and rush to the bathroom, hoping to make a kill shot. From there he would dash to the Mustang and make for the Tennessee countryside. That was the entirety of his plan.

He knew he was going to need some luck. King had to show up and he had to be exposed, and he had to still be exposed when Ray made it to the bathroom window ready to fire. Waiting in the chair, he became riddled with doubt. He'd been just as ready in Atlanta, lying in wait and in vain at the Ebenezer Baptist Church and at King's home. King might have already moved out of the Lorraine. He might come and go without being seen. Ray might see him but but not have a shot. He might have a shot and miss him. Suddenly his focus, his intention, his psycho-cybernetic certainty abandoned him, and he was sure that he would fail again. And just as suddenly, the door to room 306 opened. It was five minutes before six.

Two black men stepped out onto the balcony, a tall man in a suit, and a shorter and somewhat older one in white shirt sleeves and a striped tie. Through the binoculars Ray immediately recognized that the shorter man was King. He rushed to the door and lifted the blanketed rifle, awkwardly holding it against his body with his left arm. In one motion he opened the door with his right hand and grabbed the binoculars. He rushed down the hall and made it to the bathroom unseen, locking the door behind him.

Inside, he was hyperventilating, his heart racing like a rabbit's. He pushed the bedspread aside and lifted the

Remington GameMaster out of its box. Reaching for the cartridges, he dropped the cardboard container, the contents tumbling onto the linoleum. When he picked one up, his trembling hand dropped it among the others. There was no time to waste, this might be his only chance. He picked up the fallen cartridge, his hand still shaking, and managed to load it into the magazine. He abandoned the others. He would try this with a single shot.

Ray lifted the bathroom window hard, jamming it five inches above the sill. He was relieved at the sight of both men still on the balcony, that he still had a chance. Seeing that the best angle to King would be from the claw foot tub, he stepped in. He knew that he had perhaps only seconds to stabilize himself, to brace himself physically and mentally. At any moment King might go back inside.

For stability, Ray, standing in the tub, pinned his left shoulder hard into the wall while letting the window sill support the barrel, the muzzle protruding only a few inches beyond the ledge. He looked through the scope and saw both men, the taller one talking to King, while King's attention seemed to be focused on the parking lot below. Ray took two deep breaths and released the safety. "Do the thing and you will have the power."

The taller man was no longer visible in the scope and King, leaning forward with both hands on the railing, was still talking to whoever was in the parking lot. Ray shifted the downward angle of the Remington and moved it slightly to the left until the crosshairs of the scope were in the middle of King's face. The rifle was stable. He squeezed the trigger. It was 6:01 P.M.

The Remington-Peters .30-06 soft-pointed bullet, traveling a half a mile a second, struck King on the right side of the face, close to the corner of his mouth. Mushrooming on contact, it shattered his jawbone, destroyed his vertebral artery and jugular vein, broke his neck, and completely severed his spinal cord. Before his body struck the balcony's concrete surface, the Reverend Martin Luther King, Jr.'s prospects were no better than if he'd been decapitated.

Part Three

The News

"Good evening. Doctor Martin Luther King, the apostle of nonviolence in the civil rights movement, has been shot to death in Memphis, Tennessee."

The newscaster was Walter Cronkite, America's trusted town crier, always there for the biggest moments—space shots and war, national elections, the passing of icons. "Police have issued an all-points bulletin for a well-dressed white man seen running from the scene."

Nick had been warming up some leftover pizza in the barracks kitchen when Jeff shouted him into the living room. "Get in here," he said. "you're not gonna believe this."

"Doctor King was standing on the balcony of a second floor hotel room tonight when, according to a companion, a shot was fired from across the street," Cronkite said. "In the friend's words, the bullet exploded in his face."

It was the familiar Cronkite baritone, crisp and

authoritative, musically paced, but he read it eyes down from a sheet of paper. The famed journalist had apparently decided that the news was too important and urgent to wait for a prepared teleprompter.

"Police, who had been keeping a close watch over the Nobel Peace Prize winner because of the turbulent racial situation in Memphis, were on the scene almost immediately," he said. "They rushed the 39 year-old Negro leader to a hospital where he died of a bullet wound in the neck. The police said they found a high-powered hunting rifle about a block from the hotel, but it was not immediately identified as the murder weapon."

Nick stared at the TV set, not in disbelief but in a blur of sadness and fatalism. This is what happens, he thought, this is what always happens.

"Mayor Henry Loeb has reinstated the dusk to dawn curfew imposed on the city last week when a march led by Doctor King erupted in violence," Cronkite said. "Governor Buford Ellington has called out four thousand National Guardsmen. The police report that the murder has touched off sporadic acts of violence in a Negro section of the city. In a nationwide television address, President Johnson expressed the nation's shock."

They cut to LBJ, in black and white standing at a microphone. "America is shocked and saddened by the brutal slaying tonight of Doctor Martin Luther King," the President said. "I ask every citizen to reject the blind violence that has struck Doctor King, who lived by nonviolence."

Jeff started to say something about Johnson, but Nick shushed him. Cronkite was talking again. "Doctor King had returned to Memphis only yesterday," he said, "determined to prove that he could lead a peaceful mass march in support of striking sanitation workers, most of whom are Negro. There was shock in Harlem tonight when word of Doctor King's murder reached the nation's largest Negro community. Men, women and children poured into the streets. They appeared dazed, many were crying. A young Negro said, 'Doctor King didn't really have to go back to Memphis. Maybe he wanted to prove something.'"

The two medical students sat side-by-side in silence until Jeff, a casual Catholic, uttered the name of his putative savior.

"He lived here, you know," Nick said. "A couple years ago King had an apartment on the West Side, not far from my grandparents' deli on Roosevelt Road. You remember? He was raising hell about housing in all-white neighborhoods like Bridgeport. Didn't help that the mayor grew up there."

"What do you think's gonna happen?"

"What do you mean?"

"Well," Jeff said, "they've called out the National Guard in Memphis. What do you think's gonna happen here?"

Nick knew that there'd been large scale inner-city violence all decade long in America—in Detroit, in Newark, in Chicago itself. Watts was the worst, with dozens of deaths and tens of millions in property damage. And none of these was incited by anything as incendiary as the assassination of King.

"What do I think's gonna happen," Nick said, "I think this city is going to fucking explode."

The front door opened. It was Fisher and Plunkett, just back from a case on the South Side. "You know what's going on?" Jeff asked them.

"Yeah, we just heard about it from the cab driver who brought us here," Fisher said. "He was crying, an old black gentleman, probably in his sixties. He says, 'You boys best be careful.'"

"You guys notice anything happening out there," Nick asked, "violence, looting, anything?"

"Actually it's kind of eerie quiet," Plunkett said. "Calm before the storm maybe?"

"I wouldn't bet on maybe," Nick said.

Jeff asked if anyone knew where Larry Berlin was.

"Out on a case, I think," Fisher said. "He was next up when we left."

The four of them sat down to watch the news coverage, switching between the three networks and WGN, the local Chicago station. Reporters, one after another, summarized what little was known about the shooting. There were photos of the Lorraine Motel and there was live coverage outside of St. Joseph's Hospital, where King had been pronounced dead.

There were reports of street violence in Memphis and Los Angeles. WGN had a police official describing broken windows and looting on West Madison Street, a few miles from the Maternity Center. Each of the stations stitched together highlights of King's accomplishments—the March on Washington, the Civil Rights Act, Selma and Birmingham, the Voting Rights Act, the Nobel Peace Prize.

In less than an hour, regardless of the channel, the

coverage was repeating itself—the shooting, the Memphis photos, the King biography, LBJ's mournful plea for civility. Nick was disheartened and exhausted, and about to get to bed when the phone rang. Jeff answered it.

"Hello…yes, Doctor Butler." This got everyone's attention. "Okay…right…I understand…It certainly makes sense to me…All right, so you'll call tomorrow morning?… uh huh..Doctor Butler, do you know where Larry Berlin is?…Okay, great….Thanks…Goodbye."

"She's shutting us down for the time being," Jeff said, "sending everything to Cook County. Maybe start up again tomorrow if the city's calm. She said we should just sit tight and stay inside. That's it. Oh, and Berlin's at the Center. He'll stay there tonight."

Nick was relieved. If he didn't go out on one more case it would be just fine. There were only two full days left in the rotation, maybe he would get away without having to do another one. As he was about to get up to go to his room, there was Bobby Kennedy on the TV, in a suit and tie standing on a flatbed truck. A banner at the bottom of the screen read "Indianapolis, Indiana."

"Martin Luther King dedicated his life to love and to justice between fellow human beings," the senator said. "He died in the cause of that effort. In this difficult day, in this difficult time for the United States, it's perhaps well to ask what kind of a nation we are and what direction we want to move in. For those of you who are Black and are tempted to be filled with hatred and mistrust of the injustice of such an act, against all white people, I would only say that I can also feel in my own heart the same kind of feeling. I had a member of my family killed, but he was killed by a white man."

That memory had been competing for Nick's attention from the first mention of the King killing, intruding on the details of Memphis and the panorama of the civil rights leader's life. Seeing and hearing Bobby, his look, that particular voice, served only to remove him further from the day's tragedy, his awareness flooded with the detail of that other dreadful day, that cold and rainy November Friday. When he finally made it to bed, as tired as he was he couldn't get to sleep. He let his awareness go, and it traveled—a half a decade back and half way to Kentucky.

He was slow-walking the windy Quadrangle at the University of Illinois. Its elm trees, all of them, had been cut to stumps, leaving the pedestrians—the students, faculty, staff, the visitors—on their own against the formidable northerlies. He'd first heard about Dutch Elm Disease two years earlier at freshman orientation. The Elm Bark Beetle— an eighth-of-an-incher that flies—carries the fungus from tree to tree, unstoppable. So to save the forest, you destroy the forest and the little bugs and the moldy perpetrator, and you start over. The epidemic, a not very distant cousin of the Irish potato famine, had directly or indirectly killed every elm tree in Urbana, Illinois.

No doubt the meteorologists would have had a bloodless explanation for the north wind that swept down the Quad that night. An impoetic local phenomenon, "a column of low pressure aggregating over the north central part of the state." But on Nick's face it felt like those very molecules had begun their journey over the Arctic ice pack, roared down the prairie provinces, gave as good as they got from the floes on Lakes Superior and Michigan, dropped every last leaf from Chicago's autumnal canopy, and finally whistled their way across the finished corn fields to sting his eyes, his nostrils, his cheekbones.

It had rained hard all day, the hardest in months, and then it slowed to a drizzle at nightfall. He didn't bother with an umbrella because there was a hood on his loden coat. Alone, he leaned into the wet wind.

The Quadrangle, the architectural dead center of the University of Illinois at Champaign-Urbana, occupied ten square blocks, five north-south and two east-west. Nick was in the southeast corner, hood up, heading slowly north without a destination or a deadline. For a Friday night it was quiet. There were plenty of people, but no boisterous clusters. Mostly alone or in couples, unhurried like him, umbrella'd or hooded or indifferent.

Though it wasn't quite winter, the light, what little there was, was Midwest winter gray. The slow moving overhead matte was just thin enough that he could make out a waxing crescent moon to the east, off his right shoulder. Electric light illuminated the drizzle every hundred feet or so, from glass and metal lanterns atop twelve foot poles. And frosty glass globes softly lit the porticos and facades of the surrounding buildings.

Everything looked like it always looked, yet everything had changed.

If there was a unifying element to the Quadrangle, it

was the masonry. You could age the buildings by their complexion, the texture and deepening redness of the bricks, though at night in the rain they were just a few more shades of gray.

Nick continued slowly up the eastern side of the Quad, the big grassy mall to his left and Davenport Hall with its antebellum pillars on his right. Most of the passersby, particularly the ones who were walking alone, did something —a nod, a shake of the head, a grim smile. Aloof the day before, complete strangers, now they were family, bonded in sickening circumstance.

The next building was the most alien, and not simply because Pre-Med Organic Chemistry had been daunting, a near embarrassment. Noyes Laboratory stunk. Its gothic entry heralded the repellant by-products of the place. The scores of chimneys ringing the roof were inadequate to their task, so the air burned acrid with acid vapor, nitric and hydrochloric. And worse, with the stomach-turning reek of hydrogen sulfide. Even with the gusting northerlies, the rotten-egg stench of Noyes quickened his step.

He turned his back to the smelly laboratory and walked west along the length of the Illini Student Union, the Georgian reconstruction which formed most of the upper boundary of the Quadrangle. On its slate roof, above a long row of white dormers, was a transplanted old cupola with a bell and a clock. It was almost ten.

There were many more people walking near the Union. Still mostly in ones and twos, though, and with that familiarity of shared sadness.

Three days earlier, this was joyful ground. They'd built

a stage extending into the Quad from the south facade of the Union building. The temporary platform, adorned in a season's worth of orange, white and blue bunting, was large enough for the football team, the cheerleaders, the Fighting Illini marching band, and a gaggle of coaches and trainers and deans and faculty and local alumni. The giddy student body—there must have been twenty thousand of them—spilled all the way back to the English Building, half the length of the Quad. It was the biggest pep rally he'd ever seen. Their team was headed for East Lansing to play Michigan State for the Big Ten title and a trip to the Rose Bowl. Or so they thought.

As he walked beyond the Union to the northwest corner of the Quadrangle, he could see that something was happening just ahead. The south wall of Altgeld Hall was awash in shimmering light. This building, the home of the mathematics faculty, was like no other on campus. With its weathered gray stone blocks, gothic arches throughout and a spired bell tower, it could have been an Anglican church on eighteenth century soil.

In the concrete courtyard next to Altgeld, amid the bicycle racks and shrubbery, a makeshift congregation stood silent. Young and older, sheltered from the north wind, with flowers or lit candles or empty-handed. Nick's arrival made maybe thirty of them, then three or four more trickled in and a few fell away. A red-eyed girl in a long black raincoat offered him her candle. He took it and she lit another for herself. No one led, or even spoke.

A grad student he recognized, a T.A. from the anatomy labs, was standing by himself. The rest were strangers. An older couple, faculty he figured, stood side-by-side, their arms around each other's waists. Two other couples held hands. A young woman crossed herself and walked away. Another added her bouquet to a pile of flowers lying on the concrete. He looked from one face to the next, candlelight aflicker on sorrow.

He closed his eyes and listened to the rain, the click of footsteps, someone sobbing behind him. The ache in his throat—it had been there for hours—was suddenly worse. He swallowed hard and the tears came, rolling warm down his cheeks, then cold, evaporating into the chill. He had not cried since grammar school.

Nine hours earlier, the news was undigestible, suffocating. Headshot, then dying, then dead, their beautiful young president, their American prince. Before Ruby, before Zapruder, before the Warren Commission, before speculation. Just grief, burning. And though he didn't comprehend it that evening, and wouldn't for years to come, it was his sweet, safe Midwestern childhood's bitter end.

Rampage

Nick awoke on Friday morning to the distant wail of sirens.

The night had been fitful, his sleepless intervals inhabited by King and JFK and Sonny too. Thursday night's news from Memphis had distracted him from what happened only a few hours earlier. But in the wakeful spaces he relived his intimidation at the hands of the Abrafo gang member. Embarrassed, he'd told no one about it.

Downstairs he found his three colleagues immersed in the local TV news.

"Pack your stuff," Jeff told him, "Ernie's picking us up at noon."

"Picking who up at noon?" Nick asked.

"All of us. Their moving us to the Center. For our safety, Butler says."

"Is it that bad?"

"Watch," Jeff said, nodding toward the television set.

The shaky footage showed mobs on the street and on the sidewalks, hurling rocks through storefront windows and exiting stores with merchandise large and small. Flames leapt from garbage cans and car windows were smashed. The caption across the bottom of the screen read "West Madison Street."

"This has been going on since last night," Plunkett said, "mainly on Madison and on Roosevelt Road. Police say the mobs are getting bigger."

Madison Street was a mile and a half to the north of the barracks, but Roosevelt Road was only two blocks away. Nick was thinking about Barron's, where he'd been the day before with Ernie. It was at Roosevelt and St. Louis Avenue, in the center of the storm.

"Are we getting outta here?" Nick asked.

"I told you," Jeff said. "Ernie's picking us up and taking us over to the Center."

"No, I mean out of here." Nick was over-enunciating. "Completely out of here. Out of the inner city. Is there some kind of an evacuation plan?"

No one answered. Nick shook his head and went into the kitchen. He emptied the remains of a box of Wheaties and sat down at the dinner table, away from the TV. He was roiling, shifting in his chair, his thoughts unfinished, careening one to the next. Resting his elbows on the table, he leaned forward, eyes closed, his face in his hands.

"You okay?" Jeff startled him.

"Not really."

"Look, we'll probably all be home by tonight," Jeff said. "This whole thing'll be over."

"You know, this is just nuts," Nick said. "We're here to deliver babies and next thing you know we're next door to a fucking race riot. I don't know about you, but I'm scared."

"Hey, we're all scared. We'd be crazy if we weren't."

Nick diverted his attention to his cereal. After a few mouthfuls, he changed direction. "Have you noticed that nobody's talking about King."

"Whaddaya mean," Jeff said, "they've been constantly talking about King, about his accomplishments. Every half hour, it's the biography again."

"No, no, I meant we're not talking about him. Why's that?"

"I don't know. Like you said, a race riot down the block is a pretty big distraction."

"Truth is," Nick said, "I thought more about Kennedy last night than I did about King. I admire him, but this didn't affect me like the news about Kennedy. Just didn't. For these people it has to be beyond painful. Excruciating."

"I'm sure that's right," Jeff said.

They sat without speaking, the TV droning, Nick pushing his Wheaties around the bowl. His throat tightened and he realized that he was at the edge of tears. "Look," he said, "I better call my mother. She's probably going out of her mind. I know I am."

"Nicky, are you all right? We've been worried sick."

He was upstairs, out of earshot of the others, and decidedly not all right. "I'm fine, mom. We're safe. They've cancelled everything. All the patients are being diverted to the hospitals. We're staying inside."

"Where are you exactly?"

"We're at the residence, Booth House, the place we call the barracks. In a little while, they'll be picking us up and taking us over to the Center."

"The things we're seeing on TV are horrible," she said. "They say there's rioting on Roosevelt Road. Aren't you right there?"

Her questions were precisely his own. "I think that's west of us. Anyway, the streets around us are quiet. Really."

"Well, what's going to happen? They can't just leave you there."

"We're gonna find out in a little while. Right now I don't know any more than I've told you. Main thing is, we're safe. And I'll stay in touch. Okay?"

"This isn't right. They should be getting you out of there. Police escort, whatever it takes."

You're fucking right they should be getting us out of here.

"Mom, I'm absolutely certain that there'll be a plan to get us home. I just don't know what it is yet. I promise I'll keep in touch. You'll know when I know."

Off the phone, he grabbed his duffel bag and stuffed it, at first with some sense of order and neatness and then with abandon—the Hudson Bay blanket, his clothes, clean and dirty, his toiletries, assorted books and papers.

The only remaining item was on the bedside table, Blossom's drawing of him in his white doctor jacket, stethoscope adangle. He went back into the duffel, found a spiral notebook, and carefully placed the drawing flat between its pages.

⟡

By the afternoon, the West Side was a battle zone and getting worse.

Ernie had driven the four of them over to the Center, and they, along with nearly everyone in the building, were in the big second floor conference room following the chaos on television. Nick and Jeff were on a couch against the back wall.

"Jesus," Nick said, "this looks like a made-for-TV movie."

A fireman in full gear said, "They're walking west and burning as they go." A newscaster on the local NBC station gave an update. "We're told that as of four o'clock there are 26 major fires burning. It appears that the arsonists are following behind the swarms of looters, mostly on Madison Street, but on other commercial streets as well." A police spokesman said that ten thousand officers were being tasked to restore order, and that the mayor had asked Governor Kerner for National Guard reservists and President Johnson for troops from Fort Sheridan.

The still photos and video reminded Nick of the images he'd seen of the Watts riots three years earlier. Flames and smoke belching from commercial buildings and tenements, violent mobs of mostly young black men rampaging on the streets, smashed store fronts, scattered bodies, officers in riot gear, armored vehicles.

"This is fucking surreal," Nick murmured to no one in particular.

Doctor Butler made her first appearance since they'd come over from the barracks. She strode in, turned off the TV and gestured for quiet. "I've been on the phone for the last half hour," she said. "I've spoken with the police, with the folks at Cook County and Mount Sinai, and with the Dean. Things are obviously getting much worse. We're of course closed and we're going to stay closed until further notice. We're going to evacuate this place. Everything will be diverted to the hospitals."

Letting the announcement sink in, she lit up a Chesterfield. "No surprise, people, the police and fire departments are overwhelmed. They can't promise us anything. So here's the plan. Ernie and I are going to each take one carload at a time downtown. The police are telling me that it's quiet there and nearly empty. We'll drive south, then circle east to Lake Shore Drive and come back the same way. The drop-off will be the Northwestern train station. The riots are nowhere near there and the police assured me that the location is secure. You'll be able to wait inside. It's warm, there's food. Your friends or family can pick you up there, or you can use the local trains and connect to the CTA. It's a safe location. Taxis are supposedly operating outside of the riot areas, but I wouldn't rely on them."

Butler scanned the room, leaving space for questions but not soliciting them. She was leading, and from the silence it was apparent the group was content to follow. At least no one was speaking up. "We're going to start with the nursing students, they're by far the largest group," she said, "then the administrative staff, then the nurses and medical staff, including the medical students." She looked up at the wall clock. "I'm hoping we can complete this by eight o'clock." It was a little before five. "Ernie'll take the first group in ten minutes."

Nick was fourth in line to use a telephone in the reception area when he heard Mary behind him. "You have a call. It came in on the nursing line."

"Hello?"

"Nicky, we thought we'd have heard from you by now. Do you have any idea how worried we are? It's getting worse and worse out there. Tell me what's happening."

"Mom, I was just about to call you. Everyone's trying to call out, there's people waiting in line for the phone."

"All right. So what's happening?"

"Well, that's why I was trying to call. We're evacuating the Center and there's a plan. Can you or dad pick me up from the Northwestern train station, probably in two or three hours?"

"Is it safe there?"

"The police say it's completely safe there."

"How are you going to get there?"

"There's a plan for that, and a safe driving route. I just need for you to come down and get me at the train station. I'll call you when I get there. Can you do that?"

"This is really scaring us, Nicky. I don't like this at all."

"Mom, how do you think we feel? Just tell me, will you be able pick me up?"

"Of course we'll pick you up. You said in two hours, right?"

"They think it'll be two to three hours. I can't completely control that. I'll call as soon as I get to the train station, okay?"

"Well, if it gets longer, please call and let us know."

"I will. I promise."

Inside for hours, Nick needed a break from the repetitive television coverage and the waiting. From the space between the Center's double front doors, he looked through the glass at Halsted Street, nearly deserted at dusk. Unbundled, he stepped out and was surprised at the air temperature, fortyish, and the improbable gentleness of the wind.

The sirens, which had been muted indoors, screamed from the north and the west, layers of wailing, continuous and dissonant, the sound of a city saturated in emergency. An occasional vehicle drove by—a blue and white cop car with its flashing ruby lights, a fire truck, a jeep with a mounted machine gun. There were fewer parked cars than usual, but Sonny's was there in the same spot as the day before, a disquieting reminder of Nick's vulnerability, as if he needed one.

The sky to the northwest was aflame—reds and oranges and yellows, shimmering, aglow from the fires. A horrible beauty, he thought. He was struck by the strangeness of it, the hatred at the heart of it. He wondered if this was how war felt.

It was almost eight o'clock and two-thirds of the people were gone, on their way home. On each return for the next group of evacuees, the reports from Butler and Ernie were the same—the route was safe, nearly deserted, the train station was quiet. The plan was working.

Nick was ready to go, scheduled for the next group, on his way in about twenty minutes, he thought. The wall clock, mounted above the television in the conference room, was the kind that clicked off one minute at a time, and each minute felt like ten.

The national news coverage alternated between Chicago and the other cities that were exploding—Memphis, Baltimore, Washington, D.C. The local affiliates painted a picture of pandemonium on the West Side. Forty-some major fires now, mobs that looked two or three times larger than a few hours earlier, the police describing 28 blocks of Madison Street under siege. There were deaths, though no one was speculating on the numbers, and hundreds injured or burned.

A police official appeared on the TV reading a prepared statement. "The Mayor has issued the following to Chicago police officers," he said. "They are authorized to shoot to disable persons committing property crimes such as looting and breaking and entering, and they are authorized to shoot to kill persons assaulting civilians or law enforcement personnel. These authorizations are effective immediately."

The conference room looked like a bus station waiting room, the remaining staff and students scattered on chairs and couches, their suitcases, duffel bags and backpacks at their feet. Disbelief and agitation had given way to a collective trance—everyone staring at the television set, barely speaking, and then in murmurs and whispers.

Nick closed his eyes and drifted, hoping to dissolve the few remaining minutes. He thought about *The Secret War of Harry Frigg*, a goofy Paul Newman war comedy that he'd seen a few weeks before the rotation started. And he thought about the Cubs, whose season was about to begin.

"Nick." His shoulder was being gently shaken. "Nick."

It was Mary. "Telephone for you."

"Oh god, this is driving my mother crazy."

"It's not your mother," Mary said. "It's Caroline Amos, Blossom's sister. Blossom's in labor, her water broke an hour ago. They've been trying to get an ambulance, but no one's responding."

Labor Day

It was as if a switch were thrown in Nick's body, flooding him with adrenaline and its chemical cousins, the stuff of emergency, of fight or flight. The prospect of running, of abandoning Blossom, was wrenching. Like it or not, he'd become that family's lifeline, the only one, aside from Mary, who even knew they urgently needed help.

There were five lines on the Medical Director's desk phone, and he was working all of them. With Butler out evacuating staff and students, he'd commandeered her office hoping that somehow, amid the pandemonium consuming the West Side, he could persuade someone to dispatch an ambulance for Blossom.

He dialed and redialed the operator on the first line. On two others he was on hold for the Lawndale fire and police stations. On the fourth he was trying to reach the Cook County Hospital Emergency Room, hoping they might be able to help. The last phone line was for Caroline Amos.

He'd asked her to check in every ten minutes.

Mary was in a corner alcove on a second telephone. She was also trying and re-trying the operator and the fire department, getting either an endless hold or a disconnect.

Nick got through somehow to Cook County. A harried emergency room doc described hundreds of patients waiting to be seen, one ambulance after another disgorging as many as four burned or injured people at a time. An ambulance run for Blossom was out of the question.

Caroline called. "Blossom wants to push," she said, "and I'm telling her not to. Nobody's answering the phones, nobody's comin'. I know it's out of control out there, but we need help."

"You're doing the right thing," Nick said. "Absolutely, tell her not to push. We're doing everything we can to get an ambulance over there. How close are her contractions?"

"Every five minutes, maybe less."

"I know her water broke, is she bleeding at all?"

"No, not that I can tell, but she's hurting and I'm really scared."

Nick was startled by three sharp raps on the open office door. He looked up to see Ernie, filling most of the doorway. "You comin'?" Ernie said. "I got a carload for the train station, everyone but you. We need to go."

"Caroline, can you hold for a second? Ernie, take someone else who's ready to leave. I'll go with the next group, okay? Sorry Caroline. Look, call me in another ten minutes, all right?"

Nick took a moment to try to calm down. Eyes closed, he rested his head on Butler's desk and slowed his breathing.

This isn't working and it's not going to, he told himself. I'm going through the motions so I can tell myself that I did what I could, but I haven't. He thought about his *zayde*, about having a moral compass. You've got to know which way is north.

He'd had the idea as soon as he heard Blossom was in labor. It was a long shot and it was dangerous, and anyway Butler would never permit it. But he thought about it again after talking to the Cook County doc, and here it was again, insistent, the only thing he could think of, the only way north.

He thought about his mother, who would be horrified if she knew what he was considering. He would call her, he would reassure her, he would lie.

"Mary," Nick said, "we're wasting time on the phones, and there is no time. I have a plan, or at least a possibility. I need your help, but I'll completely understand if you say no. Thing is, Blossom can't wait. It has to happen right now."

They made it safely from the street to the sidewalk, into the building, up the stairs and to the front door of the apartment, Nick in a white medical student jacket squeezed over his down vest, a stethoscope around his neck, Mary bundled in a long wool coat. Each carried a leather equipment bag. He knocked and waited, then knocked again. The door swung open. There were a few seconds of silent and bewildered eye contact, enough time for Nick to wonder if he'd made an epic miscalculation.

"Are you out of your fuckin' mind," Sonny finally said.

"Are you just crazy or stupid or what."

"All of the above maybe," Nick said, "but we need your help, and we need it now." Suffocating in his nervousness, he barely got the words out.

"You are nuts. Don't you know what's goin' on? You got some kinda death wish? What the fuck are you thinkin', man."

As physically imposing as Sonny was—tall, black as anthracite, his cut physique barely contained in a badass tank top—Nick was relieved. Sonny was surprised and agitated but not aggressive. Even protective, it seemed.

"Look," Nick said, "I know this seems crazy, but we need your help and there's no time to waste. A patient of ours, a fourteen year-old, is in labor with twins, and it's a complicated labor, and there are no available ambulances. We're asking you—no, we're begging you—to drive us to go get her and take her to the hospital. It's a car trip, that's it. But it's got to be right now."

"Why the fuck are you askin' me? Why not somebody from your center. Why should I stick my neck out? People are gettin' killed out there."

"They've shut us down, Sonny. I can't even tell them we're doing this. And anyway, the center's cars are being used for evacuation."

"And if it's just a car trip, what are those for?" Sonny said, pointing to the equipment bags.

"We always take 'em. Just being cautious."

"Why are you doin' this? Your place is closed down and you're puttin' yourself and this nurse in danger for some ghetto girl? And you want me to help you? Why the hell are you doin' this?"

"Because I promised this girl that I'd be there for her," Nick said.

"You promised."

"Yeah, I promised."

"Jesus fucking Christ."

"Sonny, you should do it." It was his sister Freddie, walking into the room in her housecoat holding her new-born daughter. "These are good people and they're trying to take care of somebody like me, only it sounds like this girl needs them way more than I did. You should help them."

Nick watched as Sonny, gazing at his sister and niece, softened, his posture, his game face. "I must be outta my fuckin' mind."

"There's no time," Nick said, "We've gotta go."

"Where does this girl live?"

Nick remembered someone telling him that cars like Sonny's were called suicide convertibles. It had something to do with the way the rear doors were hinged, but he couldn't make sense of it. Less mysterious, though, was the timing of his recollection.

He was riding shotgun, up front on the right, watching Sonny navigate the nearly empty roads of the West Side. Mary was in the spacious back seat along with the equipment bags. Nick realized that he was no longer aware of the sirens, the din so persistent that it dissolved in its sameness. The sky was another matter, flickering orange and yellow and red, an unholy aurora.

Sonny's route made perfect sense, Nick thought, going with the expressways, the Dan Ryan and the Eisenhower, staying off the surface streets until he had no choice. They were westbound on the Eisenhower, going for the Garfield Park exit, he figured, getting them within a mile of Blossom. Sonny took the ramp, and once he was on it, it was too late.

At the top of the rise, where the ramp met Congress Street at the edge of the park, there was a barricade of police cars, four of them with cherry tops flashing. Two officers in riot gear, vests and baby blue helmets, walked shoulder to shoulder in the path of the Lincoln, gesturing 'halt' with their hands. Sonny slowed to a crawl, and even before he was at a full stop he lay both of his hands, palms up, on the dash in full view of the police. Nick was certain that this was not the first time Sonny had done this very thing.

The officers separated, one to the driver's side, the other to Nick's. Sonny was waved out of the car. "What the hell are you doing here?" the cop said. "You must know what's going on. And what the hell are you doing with these people?"

Nick slid toward the open door and said, "Officer, I can explain."

"I'm not talking to you, I'm talking to him."

"I'm sorry," Nick said, "but we've got a unique medical situation here and it's an emergency."

Apparently thinking that Mary was the patient, the officer leaned in and asked her if she was okay. "I'm fine," she said, "I'm a nurse. Would you please listen to what this doctor has to say?"

The officer relented and Nick, in a fevered summary,

explained their rescue mission.

"I understand," the officer said, "but I can't let you pass. There's a strict cordon. Nobody gets in, no exceptions. It's too dangerous."

"Did you not hear what I said? The lives of two babies, and possibly of the mother, are at stake."

"I'm sorry. I don't have the authority. I can't let you by."

"Okay, who has the authority?" Nick said, "Who can I talk to? Every minute matters. I know you have an overwhelming emergency, but this is our emergency and it's two minutes from here and we can do something about it."

He'd found a voice that he didn't know he had. He was not playing anything, acting as if he were in charge. Amid the cops in battle gear, an Abrafo gang member and a nurse who could could run circles around him as a clinician, there he was, the center of gravity.

The officer double-timed it to one of the vehicles and Nick could see him in the front seat talking on a phone. In less than a minute one of the police cars backed up, then a second one pulled to the side, opening a lane to Congress Street. The officer was waving them forward. Sonny steered the Lincoln so that the cop would be on Nick's side as they drove past. "I take it you reached someone," Nick said. "Thanks."

"Actually I didn't. Make it count."

Now Nick could see the flames, not just their reflection in the sky. As they crossed Hamlin Boulevard, the multiple fires, less than a half mile to the north on Madison Street, were easily visible from the right side of the Lincoln. He saw them again as they crossed Springfield Avenue.

"Get down, both of you," Sonny shouted. "All the way down. There's a fuckin' mob comin' at us on the right."

Nick slid down in front of his seat and Mary rolled to the floor in back. As the car sped up, he heard something strike the windshield and something else pound the right side toward the rear.

Amid the din, the roar of the Lincoln's V-8 and the dissonant whine of the sirens, there were staccato bursts, single and multiple, like popcorn popping. It was gunfire, its distance and direction impossible to gauge. It all happened faster than thought.

"We're past 'em, you two okay?" Sonny said.

"Well, I'm not injured if that's what you mean," Mary answered.

Nick said it quietly, "I'm sorry I asked you to do this."

"Not sorrier than me," Sonny said, "but we're just about there. I'm going to take the alley."

"This was too dangerous," Nick said. "I don't know what I was thinking."

"You were thinking about Blossom and her babies," Mary said, "so let's go get them."

Sonny circled to the right, doubling back up the alley running parallel to Congress Street behind Blossom's building. It looked like every other alley in the inner-city, wide enough for the garbage and delivery trucks, flanked on both sides by three and four story wooden staircases abutting Chicago's typical red-brown brick facades.

Nick pulled himself up into the seat to find the

windshield on his side cracked like a starburst. "This is it," Sonny said. Other than the Lincoln, the alley was empty. He parked as close as he could to the left, within inches of the garage opposite the back of Blossom's three floor six-flat. Before getting out and locking the car, Sonny took off his leather jacket and laid it atop the dashboard, folded with the Abrafo patch on conspicuous display.

The three of them, with Nick in the lead, climbed the wooden staircase to the third floor. Sonny had relieved Mary of one of the instrument bags, Nick had the other. After three rounds of knocking, each louder than the one before, the back door finally opened. "Thank God you're here," Caroline Amos said. She was breathless and disheveled, her pretty face wracked with desperation. This was not the composed big sister Caroline that Nick had gotten to know. "Hurry, hurry," she said, "it's happening. One foot is out and it's turning blue."

The Sticking Place

Nick had neither the luxury of time nor the availability of consultation. He tried to reach Butler for advice on where to deliver Blossom. He knew she'd be angry about his choice to ignore the shutdown, but he trusted that she'd set that aside and help him out. When he called, though, she'd just left for the train station with another carload of evacuees.

There was a decision to make and he made it. With the newborn partly delivered and in distress, it would be more dangerous to delay than to go ahead. With Mary's help he would do the breech delivery, stabilize Blossom, and head for the hospital with the second twin still in the uterus.

Writhing in pain with each contraction, and withdrawn and tearful in the spaces between, Blossom acted as if Nick were a stranger. She'd been indifferent to his arrival and more than that, overtly hostile. "Why the fuck aren't you making my pain go away," she shouted, glaring at him.

Sonny was none too happy either. "This was supposed to just be a ride to the hospital," he said. "Now you're tellin' me that you're gonna deliver this baby right here and right now. What am I supposed to do, sit around and wait for instructions? Now I'm your private fucking errand boy?"

Mary quietly asked Nick if he was certain about his decision. "As certain as I'm gonna get," he said. "Let's do it, we'll use the dining room table."

As she went into action, Nick pushed aside his disappointment over Blossom's unexpected hostility and began to mentally rehearse the breech extraction, remembering step by step the instruction he'd gotten from Grant Westerman, the senior obstetrics resident who wanted to sterilize every woman on the West Side. He was a racist prick, but he'd guided Nick through a smooth breech delivery, surprising him with his helpfulness when it counted.

The table was covered with newspaper and the instruments and supplies were ready. Caroline was in one of the bedrooms keeping her boys out of the way. Nick stepped into the living room and asked Sonny if he would help.

"What do you want me to do?" Sonny asked, irritated but apparently resigned to the situation.

"You can help me move Blossom from the bedroom to the dining room," Nick said. "Come on."

After an introduction that Blossom listlessly ignored, Sonny picked her up as if she were weightless and carried her body across his, gently setting her on the layer of newspapers.

Nick and Mary went to work. They had, in less than two weeks, become a functional team. He respected and trusted her, and she, despite his inexperience, consistently demonstrated that she believed in him. She'd told him, and it wasn't the first time that he heard it, that his competence far outdistanced his confidence.

He watched her take Blossom's blood pressure and then repeat it. He was accustomed to Mary's evident stoicism, a countenance that gave away little. But he could tell by the subtle squint, the tightness around her mouth, that something was wrong. "What?" he asked.

"Let me do this one more time." He watched her inflate and then deflate the cuff, listening intently with her eyes closed. Then she asked Nick to try it.

He did it twice and said, "I get 240 over 160."

"That's what I got," Mary said, "all three times."

"Set up the IV and get out the mag sulfate." Without discussion, they both knew what this was. Toxemia of pregnancy with high blood pressure off the charts. "Let's give her 5 grams in a quarter of a liter of saline," he said, "as fast as it'll run."

As Mary began prepping the skin around Blossom's genital area, the pungent smell of Betadine filled Nick's nose and mouth and sickened him. He'd smelled it hundreds of times, in operating rooms, emergency rooms and surgical clinics, but this time it was different. He was on the edge of running into the kitchen to throw up in the sink. Accompanying his nausea was the thought, acquired only in the last few minutes, that Blossom might die in his care.

Forget everything else, he told himself. Forget Blossom's anger, she's a fourteen year-old acting like a six year-old, awash in pain and fear. Forget Sonny's badass presence, he's not going to hurt you. Forget the hypertension, you've treated it. Forget Butler, forget your mother. You'll deal with them later. Right now there is only this breech baby. Focus. Deliver this baby and get Blossom to the hospital.

Blossom was moaning with another contraction. "Don't push yet. I know it hurts and you want to push, but don't."

"Will you fuckin' do something," Blossom shouted, "this is killin' me. I don't care. Put me out. Do somethin'." About the pain, Nick would do basically nothing. He had neither the skill nor the experience to administer an epidural or do a paracervical block. No, this would be natural child birth in the most unnatural of circumstances.

The gloves and masks were on. Nick was dead center in front of Blossom with Mary to his left. His reluctant Samaritan was back in the living room. "Sonny, would you come in here," Nick called out.

The gang member ambled into the dining room. "Now what?"

"We need your help. I'd like you to look after the boys in the bedroom so Caroline can come out here and be with Blossom."

"Yeah," Sonny said without hesitation. "I can do that."

"You wanna give her something?" Mary asked.

"Like what?"

"Demerol maybe"

Nick had been heeding Mary's suggestions from the start of the Maternity Center rotation, but not this time. "Could depress the baby's breathing," he said. "There's enough risk as it is."

He touched the baby's foot. It was magenta, and

oriented with the heel up and the toes pointed down, the advantageous position for a breech extraction. Visualizing the delivery he'd done with Westerman, he held the infant's protruding right foot with his gloved right hand and inserted his left index and middle fingers into the vagina in search of the left foot. "Don't have it," he told Mary. Reaching forward, he swept his fingers down the baby's belly and collided with what felt like a flexed knee. Sliding down from there he found the foot and grabbed it between his two fingers, pulling it out through the labia, where it lay next to its partner. Both feet were out. That's the easy part, he thought.

"Blossom," he said. There was no response. "Blossom, I need your attention." Still nothing. Caroline was now at the head of the table, within whispering distance of her kid sister. "Caroline, I need your help. You had your babies, you know what this is like. Talk to Blossom. Keep her with me. Keep comforting her."

"I'll do my best," Caroline said.

"Okay Blossom, Caroline's here. I want you to start pushing with your contractions. We're going to deliver this baby together."

Caroline paraphrased Nick, quiet and musical at Blossom's right ear.

"Blossom, let me know when the contraction's coming," he said. "Tell me when it's coming."

The next labor pain started slow but quickly had Blossom rising off the table. Nick was pleading. "I want you to push, Blossom, push and keep pushing." Caroline soothed and whispered, to little apparent avail, as Nick wrapped a sterile towel around the baby's emerging legs. He was applying traction, bringing the child out inch by inch as Blossom, a barely contained vessel of pain and rage and fear, somehow did the work.

With the next contraction, he brought the baby—it was a girl—all the way to the shoulders. "You've got a girl, honey," Caroline said, "it's a girl." If Blossom cared, there was no sign of it. She was panting, covered in sweat, her puffy eyes awash in tears, a child herself, in her unanesthetized hell of pain and panic.

Nick was taken by the simple obvious thought. A little girl having a little girl.

When the shoulders came through, she tore. A jagged tear, fortunately not too deep or long, oozing blood at its edges, in the midline where the labia met just below the vaginal opening. He understood that this unintended and messy laceration served as an episiotomy of sorts, slightly opening the gate for the aftercoming head, its emergence the most hazardous portion of a breech delivery.

He closed his eyes for several seconds, visualizing the maneuver with Westerman at his side a week earlier, the timing and the exact position of his hands. "Mary," he said, "I want you to locate the baby's head above the pubic bone. With the next contraction, push it toward Blossom's spine. I'll be pulling from below. I hope we can do this in a single move."

He asked Blossom to tell him when she began the next contraction, but expected no answer and got none. Its onset was obvious, heralded by a blizzard of profanity. "Okay, here we go," Nick said.

He placed his right forearm under the infant's body, the legs straddling each side. Sliding his hand under the face, he gently held the tips of his fingers against the cheekbones on each side of the nose. Then he rested his left hand on the baby's upper back and hooked his index and middle fingers over the shoulders on either side of the neck.

"All right Mary, now." She pushed and he pulled and, just as he hoped, in only a few seconds the head was out. Blossom's baby was born. And just as quickly, he knew she was in trouble—flaccid, blue and not breathing.

Before the umbilical cord was cross-clamped and cut, he vigorously used towels to dry the infant and wrap her for warmth. Mary went at the nostrils and mouth with a bulb syringe, which caused choking and coughing and then, thankfully, breathing. Using a stethoscope he estimated the heart rate at about 120, a bit slow but better than he feared. Gradually her color improved from a dusky reddish-blue all the way to pink. She was moving her arms and legs, at first minimally and then vigorously. At about one minute of age she emitted a lusty gratifying yelp.

Mary applied the clamps and he cut the cord. "I'll do a quick exam on the baby," he said, "would you clean up Blossom and get her ready to go?" He did a fast head-to-toe neonatal assessment on the kitchen table with Caroline at his side. "It's grossly normal and that's good enough for now," he told Caroline. "She'll get a thorough exam at the hospital."

"Where will you take them?" Caroline asked.

"To Sinai, I think. It's the closest. I know you have to stay here with your boys. Would you do me a favor?"

"Of course, anything."

"Would you call the Maternity Center and tell Doctor Butler what's happened, and that we're taking Blossom and the baby to Mt. Sinai. And if she's not there, leave a message. Would you do that?"

"Sure. Absolutely."

"Nick," Mary called from the dining room. He didn't hear her the first time. She summoned him again, this time shouting, out of character for this mature and unflappable veteran nurse. At first sight, in his surprise and confusion, he thought somehow that it was Mary who was bleeding. The blood covering her from her waist to her knees was of course Blossom's. She was hemorrhaging from her vagina, enough bleeding, he thought, once he had his wits about him, to kill both Blossom and her unborn twin.

Sonny had Blossom in an inverted V over his shoulder like a fireman. Nick was next to him holding the IV bottle, his arm fully extended over his head. Mary was right behind them descending the wooden backstairs with the newborn in her arms. Both patients were wrapped in blankets courtesy of Caroline. The baby was wailing, Blossom was unconscious, likely in hemorrhagic shock.

The Lincoln was unmolested, maybe dumb luck, maybe its conspicuous Abrafo identity a deterrent. Nick choreographed the seating arrangement, Sonny of course behind the wheel, Mary riding shotgun with the baby. He positioned Blossom diagonally across the back seat with her head lowered nearly to the floor, this to try to maximize blood flow to her brain. He was next to her with the elevated IV bottle.

Looking at her face, her color was ghastly, a sickly gray-brown. Her eyes, puffy an hour earlier, looked sunken. Nick's free hand held her pulse at the wrist. It was rapid and weak, *thready* in the lingo of the doctors of catastrophe. He was ready, at any moment, to feel no pulse at all.

Sonny gunned the Lincoln eastbound down the alley behind Congress, standing on the horn as he approached the cross streets. There were many more rioters on the streets than earlier, but he wasn't slowing for anyone or anything. This time neither Nick nor Mary needed to be told to stay low in their seats. The Lincoln screamed around the corner at Hamlin and again on Harrison as Sonny tore for the Eisenhower eastbound on-ramp. There were fires in every direction, some looking as close as a block away. Once on the Expressway, a zone of relative safety, Nick took stock of Blossom. She was alive but still unconscious, responsive only to deep pain, hard pinching of the skin. Her breathing was shallow, her pulse unchanged.

They approached the Sacramento Avenue off-ramp, the gateway to Garfield Park and Mt. Sinai Hospital. "This time, let's hope the cops are here," Nick said.

Sonny glanced back, "Are you crazy?"

"Just let me do the talking."

When they climbed the off-ramp, it was the same routine as earlier—multiple cruisers with their lights flashing, heavily armed police in riot gear approaching the car. Nick lowered the left rear window, gathering the command that this would require.

"You can't enter this neighborhood, back down the ramp and..."

"Officer," Nick said in the loudest voice he could muster without shouting, while conspicuously displaying the IV bottle. "We're from the Chicago Maternity Center and the girl next to me is bleeding to death right now. We need an escort to Sinai. There is no time for anything else. Get one of these cruisers in front of us and get us to Sinai. Please, just do it."

The officer leaned in and apparently one look at Blossom was enough. He raced to the patrol car closest to Sacramento, had a word with the officer behind the wheel and waved the Lincoln forward. Sonny, without turning around, said, "Man, I am fuckin' impressed."

Siren screaming, lights flashing, they were at the emergency entrance of Mt. Sinai Hospital in three minutes. The scene was a chaotic crush—multiple police cruisers, ambulances, fire department vehicles, news trucks, injured people on foot, several on gurneys. Mary handed the newborn to Sonny and ran inside for a gurney for Blossom. She rolled one out and she and Nick lifted Blossom and her IV aboard. He wheeled her inside and asked the first nurse he saw, "Who's doing triage?" She pointed to a tall balding man in scrubs who looked surprisingly calm given the madness around him. He imagined that this doc had been to war—given his age, probably Korea.

"Doctor," Nick said, "this girl is bleeding to death. She's postpartum, probably a placental abruption, one twin delivered, one still inside. If you don't get her to surgery right now, she is going to die."

He looked at Nick, then at Blossom, and then back at Nick. "Who the hell are you?"

"I'm from the Chicago Maternity Center. I'm a senior Northwestern medical student and none of that matters. The only thing that matters is that you get this girl some blood and get her to the OR right now."

"You're pretty bossy for a medical student, you know."

"There's no time for bullshit. Are you gonna help her or not?"

The triage doc smiled. "I did the Maternity Center too. I like you, kid. You've got stones."

Nick took a breath. "Look, I didn't mean to be rude. This is my patient and she's dying. That's it. It's up to you. If you get her to surgery, she has a chance."

He whistled, the kind of whistle you do with your fingers in your mouth. In moments a nurse was at his side. "Get this patient in an acute room," he said, "hang some O negative blood and get the OB resident down here stat. Highest priority."

"Can I stay with her?" Nick asked.

"Suit yourself, kid."

Blossom's acute room was not a room at all but one of eight stalls separated by sliding curtains, each accommodating one dire calamity or another. Nick imagined the third degree flame burns and gunshot wounds and brain-crushing head injuries that likely lay behind those flimsy partitions.

Blossom was on the same gurney that brought her in, plugged into IV lines in both arms, one with a unit of whole blood running wide open and other with saline. A portable stack of bedside monitors followed her pulse, respirations, blood pressure and an EKG trace. The OB resident was a tall Nordic guy who was losing his patience with Nick.

"Is there an operating room opening up?" This was the fourth time in fifteen minutes that Nick, in one combination of words or another, had asked this question.

"Look," the resident said, "Blossom needs emergency surgery, and so do two dozen other patients. The head of the OR is the chief of anesthesiology and he's making the calls. He's got Blossom for the next available room. What the hell else do you want?"

Nick was exhausted and wired. He knew he was being intrusive, and that these people were doing their job. Yet there was a kind of momentum to his agitation and he was having trouble reeling it in. And there was something else that had him on edge, a piece of unfinished business that he was avoiding.

"Hey, I'm sorry," he said to the resident. "Is there a phone around here I can use?"

It was in a small windowed office in the corner of the hall of casualties. He picked up the receiver, hesitated and dialed. It was answered after the first ring. "Hello?"

"Hi mom, it's Nick. I'm sorry, I..."

"Oh my God, are you okay? Where are you? We've been worried to death. You said you were going to call hours ago."

"I know, I'm sorry. It's a long story. I'm at Mt. Sinai Hospital with a..."

"Mt. Sinai. That's in the middle of the worst of everything. Why didn't you go to the train station like you said you would?"

"Like I said, mom, it's a long story. I made a commitment to a patient, to a family, and one thing led to another. When there's time I'll tell you all about it. I think maybe you'll understand."

"Well it's hard to understand how you could let yourself be in the middle of that."

"It was a choice I made, that's all I can say."

"So when are you getting out of there? How are you getting out of there?"

"I don't know," he said, "but I'm safe here at Sinai and I'm confident that I'll find a safe way home."

"You'll call us, yes? You won't leave us in the dark again?"

"Hold on a minute." A staff of four, the OB resident in the lead, were rolling Blossom out of her stall. "Mom, I've got to go. They're moving my patient to surgery. I've got to go right now. I'll call you later." He hung up and chased the team into an elevator.

"You're headed for the OR?" he asked.

"That's right."

"I'd like to scrub in."

"You'll have to talk to the surgeon, the attending OB, about that."

"Who's the attending OB?"

"Max Levy. he's the head of the department here."

Nick found Levy at the scrub sink just outside the operating room. He could see through a glass partition that

Blossom was being prepped by the nurses. Levy was older than he expected, perhaps seventy, with a shock of white hair and watery blue eyes. His hands dripping with soap, Levy pre-empted him. "You're the medical student who brought this girl in, aren't you?"

"Yes, sir. I am."

"That's a helluva story."

"It was a hell of an experience."

"I hope you know that just because she made it here, she's not out of the woods."

"I'd like to scrub in, sir."

"Out of the question."

"May I ask why?"

"You're not on staff, obviously. Your medical school, Northwestern I take it, has no affiliation with this hospital and this ain't gonna be a teaching case. Don't have time for it, the place is a twelve alarm disaster."

"I'll just watch. No questions, I promise. I'll be a fly on the wall."

"This girl is that important to you?"

"Yes sir, she is."

He was scrubbed, capped, gowned and gloved as a matter of operating room policy, but exiled to a side wall and instructed not to speak. Levy told him, with a kindly smile, that he would be immediately tossed out of the OR if he didn't stay out of the way and keep quiet.

Nick knew from the position of the doctors and nurses around the operating table that they were going into

Blossom's abdomen. This was no surprise, an emergency Cesarean section the obvious treatment of choice. What did surprise was the speed of the delivery. He could see Levy on the side of the table opposite from where he was standing, and it was no more than two minutes from the skin incision to a limp, purple infant being lifted out of Blossom's uterus.

The cord cut, one of the nurses carried the infant to a side table on a towel. It was clear to Nick from the absence of urgency, the dignified handling, the placement of the blanket over rather than around the baby, that Twin B Amos, as she would be called, was stillborn.

This was not unexpected. Given the magnitude of Blossom's blood loss, Nick would have been surprised had the second twin survived. But his body had a reaction all its own. Suddenly light-headed and queasy, he let the wall behind him absorb his weight. He bent forward, his head between his knees, hoping he wouldn't faint or throw up. Breathe slow and deep, he told himself, breathe slow and deep.

Levy was plenty busy with Blossom, and if he noticed Nick's quiet collapse, he didn't do anything about it. No one was sent to his rescue. After a minute or so, Nick stood up straight, staying in contact with the wall for support and doing his best to recover his demeanor.

Exhausted, shaken, he watched and listened to the rest of the surgery as if he were underwater. He could see large clots of blood being scooped and lifted out of Blossom's belly. There was talk of kidney failure, of the need for more whole blood. Two units were already hanging. A very large hunk of tissue, presumably her uterus, was placed in a stainless steel pan and set aside.

He heard Levy say, "Let's close her." After a few more minutes there was the snapping of gloves coming off. A fresh team of four came in with a gurney and started the process of moving Blossom. The anesthesiologist stayed with her, using a bag and mask for ventilation.

"I'm sure you saw that the baby didn't make it." Levy had walked over to Nick, the senior surgeon giving the medical student the courtesy of a brief report. "That baby was dead for a good while, probably right from the time of the abruption and hemorrhage. The girl's a mess. We took her uterus and stopped the bleeding, but her lungs and especially her kidneys are struggling. And who knows about her brain."

"Where's she going?" Nick asked.

"To recovery, then to surgical ICU. I'll see her again in a while."

"What floor is recovery on?"

"Why do you ask?" Levy said, obviously knowing where this was headed.

"I want to follow her."

"No, and this time no means no."

"But sir I…"

"No, and no arguments." Levy said, a step closer and fixed on Nick with his striking blue eyes. "You look like shit, son. When's the last time you got some sleep? Go upstairs to the fathers' waiting room. There's some nice couches there. Go lie down before you fall down."

Rounds

He opened his eyes to rows of rectangles, Styrofoam ceiling panels interrupted here and there by unlit fluorescent arrays. The room, though, was mid-morning bright. His disorientation was fleeting, no more than a few seconds. It was Sinai, he remembered, and unless he'd slept for 36 hours, it was Saturday. Friday could easily have been a dream, a nightmare, but he knew it wasn't.

"Good morning, Weissman." The voice was unmistakable, and so was the smoke. He sat up and turned. Butler was in an upholstered chair behind him to his right. She had a paperback in one hand, the one she'd been reading at Freddie and Sonny's flat a week earlier, and a working Chesterfield in the other.

"What time is it?" Nick asked.

"A little after 11," Butler said. "You wanna get started?"

"Get started with what?"

"We've got two patients in this hospital. You want to

see them, don't you?"

He was nervous. Not about visiting Blossom and her baby, but about Butler's reaction to his mutiny, his disregard for her evacuation plan. He decided to get it over with. "Sure, I want to see them," he said. "But isn't there something else you want to talk to me about?"

"First things first," she said after a long look. "Let's make our little rounds."

She led him to a staff-only stairwell and up two flights of stairs to another restricted doorway. Following close behind, he watched her navigate the privileged route with the self-assurance that seemed to infuse everything she did. He didn't want to be in her world, not one more day, but he admired the way she moved through it.

He followed her into the surgical intensive care unit and spotted Blossom across the room, sitting partially upright amid a tangle of tubes and wires, a bank of monitors and a pair of IV stands and bottles. He saw that there was no blood hanging and thought that was a good sign. As he stepped forward, Butler held back.

At the bedside, he asked a nearby nurse if Blossom was asleep. "Well, if you can call it that," she said. "She's pretty drugged."

"Has she seen her baby?"

"Oh, no. She won't for a while."

"She's stable, right?" he said. "She seems stable."

The nurse looked past him. "You're with Doctor Butler, I take it."

"That's right. From the Maternity Center."

"What's your name?"

"Weissman."

"What's your first name?"

"It's Nick," he said. "Nicholas."

"Hmm," the nurse said. "Yeah, she's stable. We think she's gonna be okay. Do you want me to try to wake her up?"

He was surprised at his certainty, at the starkness of his depletion. He wanted, more than anything, to not be needed. "No," he said. "Let her be." He would be doctorly again, he thought, but not today.

He waited as Butler reviewed Blossom's chart, then trailed her to the elevator. On the ride up, she asked him if he was all right. "How do you mean?" he said.

"When Max Levy called me last night, he said he was worried about you, and this morning you seem, well, out of it, distracted, you tell me."

"Doctor Levy called you last night?"

"Yeah, he called me. How do you think I knew you were here at Sinai?"

"I asked Blossom's sister to call and tell you we were coming here," Nick said. "You didn't hear from her?"

"No I didn't, but I was in and out and the phones were crazy. She probably tried."

The elevator doors opened. A corridor leading to the Newborn Nursery opened onto an alcove with a couch and a chair. Butler gestured Nick to sit down, lit another cigarette, and joined him. "I'll try this again," she said, "are you okay?"

"I'm just tired, that's all."

"Are you worried that I'm angry about what you did yesterday?"

"Are you?" he asked.

"I was," she said. "It was foolish, dangerous."

"I know."

"You'd probably do it again, wouldn't you?" she said.

"Honestly, I don't know."

Butler took a drag and another. "Weissman," she said, "it's quite a thing to save a life. I've saved my share. It's quite a thing. You saved two yesterday. You don't go out there, nobody goes out there, and that teenager and both of those babies are dead. All three of them bleed to death. You know that, don't you?"

"I was lucky, we were lucky."

"Of course you were lucky. But you were also courageous and smart. Mary told me everything, all the details, everything that happened."

"Where is Mary?" he asked.

"She's home. The police gave her a ride, the same cops who gave me an escort over here."

"I need to thank her. She's been my guardian angel these last two weeks."

"She always picks one," Butler said. "I'm sure you'll be able to reach her."

Nick was feeling the end of it now, the unweighing, the shedding of obligation, of performance, of fear. It was physical, like removing a layer of wet clothing, and then another. He'd saved Blossom, and walking away from her felt like saving himself.

"Let's go see the baby," he said.

There were two sections to the nursery, one with rows of bassinettes, open little beds containing blanketed well babies, the other a cluster of isolettes, Plexiglas chambers on wheels, for the newborns requiring closer attention. A nurse led them to Blossom's daughter.

Nick was no neonatologist but he thought the infant looked good. She was smallish, maybe five pounds, breathing quietly and easily. There were no IV lines or oxygen hook-ups. She was in an isolette, he figured, for temperature control.

Standing there, he wondered if he would feel the gravity of it, that this baby was alive because of him.

She had cocoa skin, lighter than Blossom's, and a round little head. He remembered being taught that breech babies often had perfectly round heads, spared from the birth canal crush endured by head-first babies. She lay quiet, and then she startled, her arms and legs flexing in harmony before slowly settling back to where they began. He knew that this was one of the quirks of the normal newborn nervous system.

He'd intended to only observe her, but changed his mind. After scrubbing his hands, he reached through the isolette's port holes and touched her, skin-to-skin, palpating her belly and tapping at her reflexes. Butler offered a stethoscope and he took it, placing it over her heart and then her lungs. His attention, though, was not on this baby's cardiac lub-dub or the whoosh of air with each respiration.

He just wanted more of her, to touch her, to breathe her in, to feel whatever there was to feel. Waiting for a revelation, a sense of accomplishment, what he felt—in his chest, his throat, his eyes—was a wave of sadness. He sat down cross-legged on the tile floor next to the isolette and let it be. It was a blur. King and the dead twin and the blood in the streets, and Blossom and this baby alive in the hospital. Impossible, he thought, this all just seems impossible.

"Did you notice her name?" Butler asked.

"What?" he said, adrift in his inventory.

"Did you notice her name?"

He had not. It was right there taped to the front of the isolette, a pink paper rectangle inscribed in block letters with a black magic marker. It read "Amos, Twin A," and above that, in larger letters and by a different hand, "Nicole."

It took him a few moments to get it. And when he did, he looked up at Butler and managed to push the words out. "Would you take me to the train station now?" Though his eyes were blurred with tears, he thought she was looking at him the way he'd seen her softly surrender to her patients.

"No, Weissman," she said, "I'm not going to take you to the train station. I'm going to take you all the way home."

Epilogue: June

Nick was insistent and Jeff was reluctant. It was going to take at least three days to drive to San Francisco, and Jeff wanted to get a fast start. The last thing he was interested in was a side trip, much less a return to the ruins of the West Side. Nick held his ground. "Look, I just want to see the place," he said, "it won't add more than an hour."

They were in the two week hiatus between medical school graduation and the beginning of internship, Nick's in San Francisco and Jeff's in Palo Alto. Nick's Chevy Corvair was thick with suitcases, cardboard cartons and shopping bags, string-tied books and record albums. The newly minted doctors were headed west to do battle at the next level of the medical education gauntlet.

Nick had the upper hand. It was, after all, his car and he was at the wheel for the first leg of the trip. He made his way to Roosevelt Road from the Eisenhower Expressway and within a few minutes they were parked in front of Barron's.

Over two months had passed since the riots and fires, but the area still looked like a war zone, an urban landscape of tumbled bricks and fallen timbers, boarded-up windows and yellow barrier tape. From the curb, Barron's looked like the rest. The windows were gone, partially replaced by plywood. Most of the Chicago red bricks had been seared black. The big blue-lettered sign was singed and burned entirely through in three places.

The sidewalk in both directions was deserted except for a black kid who looked about ten and was sitting on the pavement leaning against the west end of the storefront.

"Can we go now?" Jeff asked, his impatience uncamouflaged. "I'm not comfortable around here."

"I'm going inside," Nick said.

"You're shitting me. Let's get outta here."

"I'll just be a minute."

Nick got out of the car and walked through the burned out entry of his *zayde's* delicatessen. The smell was an assault, pungent and bitter, irritating his nose and his eyes. This was more than the combustion of wood, he knew. This was chemical, maybe poisonous.

It was brighter inside than he expected. Looking up, he saw a ragged gaping hole that had been burned through the ceiling and the roof. The wood floor was buckled and wet from a recent rainstorm.

He'd imagined a damaged deli, charred but recognizable. Instead he found himself in an empty alien space. There was nothing left—no furniture, no fixtures, no paintings. Whatever wasn't destroyed, he figured, had been looted. It felt like an abandoned burned out warehouse. This isn't Barron's, he said to himself. There is no Barron's here.

After lingering for a minute or so, he went out the front door and headed for the car. "Hey mister," he heard the kid on the sidewalk say. "Hey mister, you gotta quarter?"

Nick kept walking, circling the front of the Corvair to the driver's side. He got in, put the key in the ignition and hesitated.

"Come on, let's go," Jeff said.

"I'm sorry," Nick said. "There's something I want to do."

"What?"

"I'll be right back."

Jeff exhaled his annoyance.

Nick got out of the car and walked up to the kid, who was standing now, leaning against the building. "What would you do with a quarter if I gave it to you?"

"I don't know. Probably get some candy."

"What's your name?" Nick asked.

"James. Jimmy."

"Do you know what this place was, Jimmy?"

"Yeah, it was some kind of restaurant."

"Did you ever eat here?"

"No, sir."

"Jimmy, this was my grandfather's restaurant. His name was Abe. It was a special place and Abe was a special man. When I was your age he used to bring me here. We'd have lunch here and he'd teach me about the business. He was always very nice to me."

"So, you gonna gimme a quarter?" Jimmy asked.

Nick reached into his pants pocket and executed an

exaggerated search the way Abe always did it. Finally, out came the coin. "Son, my grandfather gave me one of these whenever I came here and I'm giving this one to you. It's a silver dollar. He always told me to save them. You could get a lot of candy with it, but you should think about saving it."

Jimmy took the coin and said, "Thanks, mister." Then he pivoted and ran down the street. Nick stood there watching him. The kid looked back once and kept running.

Nick walked back to the car, got in and returned the key to the ignition.

"You ready to go this time?" Jeff asked.

"I am."

"You're sure?"

"Yeah, I'm sure." Nick said. "Let's go to California."

Acknowledgements

Gratitude first to my wife Gayle, who has been an enthusiastic advocate for this book since its inception over a decade ago. Her belief in its relevance and quality has been a steady source of support and encouragement. It's a lucky novelist who has a loving partner who knows her way around quality fiction.

Jessica Grant is an editorial angel. A fine writer and teacher of writing, her commitment to this novel, her generosity of time and attention, was inspiring and instrumental in getting this writer over the finish line.

David Cole at Bay Tree Publishing has been a pleasure to work with. A seasoned industry pro, he is friendly, accessible and lets me win an argument or two.

Sasha Paulsen, my editor at the *Napa Valley Register,* gave me the opportunity seven years ago to be a steady journalistic presence in my home town. Her flexibility and support have allowed me to have a local voice and the

255

protected time, when I needed it, to complete the work on this book.

This novel was enriched by input from my Northwestern University Medical School classmates, who contributed their recollections of the Chicago Maternity Center experience: Gary London, Bob Strunk, Al Robbins, Steve Embury, Bert Glader, Mitch Komaiko, Ron Greene, Jeff Klein, Neil Stone, Rich Merel and especially Tim Hunter, whose diary and photographs were invaluable.

The historical elements of the novel relied on a number of unique resources: Northwestern's Chicago Maternity Center Archive (special thanks to Susan Sacharski), the National Civil Rights Museum in Memphis, TN, the Shiloh National Military Park and Hampton Sides' *Hellhound on His Trail*, the definitive book on the odyssey of James Earl Ray.

Along the way, the manuscript was "workshopped" at the Squaw Valley Writers Conference, Piper's Frith in Newfoundland, the Napa Valley Writers Conference and at Esalen Institute with kudos to Tom Stanbauer.

A big thanks to the early believers, the people who were fans of the drafts in the aught's: Jim McManus (my original kickstarter), Bob Reece, Sharon Bowers, John Viviano, Andrew Lustig, David Marshall and Gary Crandall.

Finally, continuing gratitude to my little writers group, Beth Franks and Allie Timar, who digested and lovingly critiqued, bit by bit, the entire manuscript.

About the Author

David Kerns retired a decade ago from his career as a senior hospital executive and Stanford medical professor to devote himself full-time to writing. For the past six years he has been a columnist and feature writer for the *Napa Valley Register*. Born and educated in Chicago, his inspiration for *Fortnight on Maxwell Street* was his own two-week Northwestern medical student rite of passage at the Chicago Maternity Center on the city's West Side.

About the Cover Photograph

The front cover photograph is by award-winning Time/LIFE photographer Fritz Goro. Taken in 1954 at a Chicago Maternity Center home delivery, it was part of a large pictorial collection depicting urban decay in mid-twentieth century Chicago.